HARVEST AMERICAN
Writing

Consider This, Señora

Consider This, Señora

HARRIET DOERR

A Harvest Book
Harcourt Brace & Company
San Diego   New York   London

Requests for permission to make copies of any part of the work should be mailed to: Permissions Department, Harcourt Brace & Company, 6277 Sea Harbor Drive, Orlando, Florida 32887-6777.

"Picnic at Amapolas" and "Another Short Day in La Luz" appeared in the *New Yorker*, "Goya and the Widow Bowles" in *Epoch*, and "A Over Middle C" in the *Santa Monica Review*.

Library of Congress Cataloging-in-Publication Data
Doerr, Harriet.
Consider this, señora/Harriet Doerr. — 1st Harvest ed.
p.   cm. — (A Harvest book)
ISBN 0-15-600002-4
1. Country life — Mexico — Fiction.   2. Americans —
Mexico — Fiction.
I. Title.
[PS3554.O36C6   1994]
813'.54 — dc20   94-18888

Designed by Trina Stahl

Printed in the United States of America

First Harvest edition 1994
A B C D E

For

Mike and Martha

Ornamenta sunt mea.

—CORNELIA
Smith's Latin Lessons, 1923

Contents

Consider This, Señora

Picnic

at

Amapolas

....

A NUMBER OF years ago in the town of
La Luz, on an August day half of hot sun, half of
rain, Don Enrique Ortiz de León prepared to sell his ancestral estate to an American gentleman and an American
lady. "The economy of Mexico compels me," he explained,
facing his two buyers across a desk littered with legal briefs.
"Taxes," said Don Enrique. On the wall behind him, under
his grandmother's portrait, hung a 1962 calendar dark with
inked-out days. "Taxes," he repeated. "They are becoming
insupportable."

The American gentleman, who was using the false name
of Bud Loomis, nodded. Like other travelers, he had come
to Mexico for the sake of new surroundings, to get away.

1

Particularly to get away. His own taxes were under investigation in Arizona. In his pocket was a summons to appear in a Tucson court that day. "I know what you mean," Bud said in border Spanish. He drummed his blunt fingers on the arm of his chair and stared at Don Enrique's calendar.

"So I am selling the land that came to me through my mother—all four *hectáreas* of my land at Amapolas." As he spoke these words, Don Enrique—Don Enrique César Ortiz de León—apologized silently to that Castilian ancestor of his who had stepped just behind Cortés onto Mexican soil. He drew his spare frame taller in order to stiffen his pride.

"How large is an *hectárea*?" asked the woman in slow, precise Spanish. From her shoulder bag she removed a pencil and a notepad, on which her name, Susanna Ames, was printed at the top. She pulled her chair closer and made space at a corner of Don Enrique's crowded desk.

Susahnahahmes, Don Enrique pronounced phonetically to himself. Her name is Susahnahahmes. He repeated it like a soundless chant. In answer to her question, he said, "An *hectárea* is ten thousand square meters."

Bud Loomis, who had reduced her name to one syllable on the day they met, said, "The whole thing's ten acres, Sue, give or take." Then added, without speaking, This is going to be a steal.

"Ten acres. As much as that." She was clearly surprised.

At this, an identical notion entered the minds of both

men. They believed they were in the presence of a helpless female. This Susahnahahmes, Don Enrique supposed, was in need of a man. Perhaps one her own age, or—better—an older man, one who understood business and the law.

Bud retained his original impression of her. When he and Sue Ames had met for the first time, by coincidence, in the property agent's office, he noticed her looks and her reckless attitude toward land and concluded then that all she needed was shaping up. Further acquaintance had only reinforced his opinion.

Now, with the two men observing her, Susanna Ames began to draw for the first time in years. She sketched on her notepad a long rise of ground, which dropped to a lake at one end and met the steep slope of a hill at the other. Beyond these she drew in a whole landscape of cornfields and, beyond them, a range of mountains that climbed to a peak. She lined one shore of the lake with a neat row of houses and a church. She left empty the flat, extended surface of the rise, though she might have penciled in a dream, for in a corner of her mind that excluded reason she had already constructed a low adobe house and a separate studio looking north and had planted apricot and fig trees, a small vineyard, and an alfalfa field, simply for the green of it. Though this house did not appear on the page, Don Enrique noticed that she was exaggerating everything—the fields, the mountains, the good order of the dwellings that faced the pond. He had never seen so elegant a small church as the one that took rough shape on her page. He became concerned.

"Consider this, señora," Don Enrique said. "You are transforming Amapolas into something more beautiful than it is." Then he went on, "Have you visited the property?"

Sue continued to draw. Now, at the center of the rise, she was outlining a Stonehenge of tilting columns and broken pediments—all that was left of Don Enrique's centuries-old *hacienda*.

Don Enrique persisted. "Were you there long enough to walk about?"

Is he crazy? Bud asked himself. We've already told him we'd buy.

Sue said, "We spent an afternoon there with the agent."

Bud corrected her. "An hour and a half," he said. "Just before dark." But even in that brief period he had found time to walk about. Once satisfied in respect to connections for electricity and water, he had started pacing off the land.

On that occasion Sue Ames had gazed after his short, thick figure as it moved away, stepping out straight lines and corners in the distance. It pleased her to think that he was drawn as she was to the serene, empty place. Even so, it had taken her ten days to reach a decision. Between calls to her lawyer and her bank, Sue considered alternatives each morning on a sunny bench in the principal plaza of La Luz, each rainy evening on a stiff chair in her hotel room.

Actually, the matter had been settled the day she chose La Luz as a stopping place, partly because of the sweep of landscape that surrounded it and partly because no one she knew had recommended it. Neither her friends nor her family in California could be aware of this settlement, remote as it was from any airport and from both coasts. Sue, divorced barely a year ago, believed that in rural Mexico she might at last be let alone. People here would hardly expect her to live wisely, marry happily.

A middle-sized town of no particular architectural or archaeological interest, La Luz rested quietly on the plain between a winery on the east and a railway line on the west. Trains bound north and south stopped at the red plastered station twice a day to load and unload freight and a passenger or two. The plaza of La Luz, shaded green by Indian laurels, faced on one side the entrance to the town's main hotel. This was the Posada del Sol, a hostelry of thirty rooms, cold and bare as cells. Sue took one of these, first for three nights, then a week, and eventually, as it turned out, for a number of months.

At first her days were all alike. She sat each morning in the plaza, ate a lunch of thick soup and bread in the hotel, and spent her afternoons outside the town, driving wherever any road would take her. It may have been the intensity of light or the transparency of air or simply the illusion of unlimited space that brought her to a decision.

On her third evening at the hotel she spoke to the

manager. "I believe I will remain in Mexico," she said. "Perhaps in La Luz. Do you know of a house?"

The manager was also the owner of the hotel—a man worn thin by lack of trade. He contemplated the American woman, one of his fourteen registered guests. His examination revealed nothing, except that she appeared more determined than other women he had known, and richer. He gave her the name of the property agent whose office was around the corner, between a notions shop and a bakery.

The following morning Sue entered the agent's ground-floor room only to find someone else, a stranger, already there.

"Another American client," said the agent.

"Bud Loomis," said the man.

Sue waited on a chair against the wall for Bud to transact his business. Time went by, and it became clear to her that an impasse had been reached.

Bud finally turned away from the agent's desk. "You go ahead," he told her. "I've got to do some figuring."

Then, as though preordained, it all began to happen, step by step. Sue inquired about a house to rent, then about one to buy. She said, "But there must be something."

A silence fell, and she rose to leave. Then Bud turned from the window. He said, "Wait a minute."

Sue sat again and listened to him say, "There's a piece of land we could split up."

Before the day was over, arrangements had been made to visit the property at Amapolas. The agent requested credentials, and Bud produced a deposit slip verifying a substantial cash balance in a local bank. Sue said she would have to call her lawyer in California and also her bank. She displayed documents—a passport and a driver's license. But the agent had already noticed about her an air of absentminded integrity, which by itself inspired trust.

That was ten days ago. Now in Don Enrique's office, at the back of his high-ceilinged house, Sue went on drawing. She outlined a stand of pines behind the ruined walls.

"I have something to suggest," interposed the lawyer. "That we visit the property together, to avoid a misunderstanding. Please be my guests on Sunday. We will eat lunch in the fresh air."

"No need to bother with all that," said Bud. "We're ready to settle now."

But Sue was accepting the invitation.

"Then we will meet at Amapolas," and Don Enrique examined his two buyers. Their indifference to each other puzzled him. "You are related, are you not?" he asked. "Brother and sister?" Though this seemed impossible. There was no resemblance. "Or cousins?"

The impatient man across from him shook his head. The lovely Susahnahahmes shook hers. Don Enrique lifted a hand to warn her, a guileless woman entering into a costly negotiation with a stranger who was in a hurry. But in the end, addressing them both, he only said, "Do you have a car?" As if that, as well as the land, were something they would share. Each, however, had a car, and nodded.

"Next Sunday at two," said Don Enrique. He turned to the calendar, circled the proposed date, and at the same time crossed out yesterday's, which had slipped by unnoticed.

ON SUNDAY THE three cars converged almost simultaneously at the picnic place, having turned in close succession from the highway at a sign that said, AMAPOLAS DEL LAGO, 1 KM. Don Enrique's ancient Buick sedan, packed with baskets and folding furniture, led the way along two ruts between thickets of weeds. Still in single file, they were almost in sight of the lake when a new sign, hand lettered, appeared on their right. LOMAS DE AMAPOLAS, it read, and indicated the way across a narrow ditch and up an abrupt slope.

Bud was the first to jump out of his car, a pickup truck so new it still lacked license plates. He walked over to a huisache tree in whose sparse shade Sue had parked her station wagon, which held a number of flat wooden boxes and an easel in the back. Looking in, Bud foresaw art that would never sell. He asked if she had noticed the new sign at the turnoff.

"Lomas de Amapolas—what a name for a place to live," he said. "Poppy Heights."

Sue directed her attention to Don Enrique, who stood next to his car, offering his arm to the oldest man she had ever seen. When this person was finally on his feet outside and drawn up to his full, crooked stature, Don Enrique introduced him as Pepe Gómez, who had been born on this land and was the grandson of his own great-grandfather's majordomo. Then Don Enrique introduced the Americans to Pepe.

"These are the people who are buying the property," he informed the aged man. "Señor Loomis and Señora Susahnahahmes." Don Enrique went on to say that he and Pepe usually drove out here on Sundays. "Though I never lived here, this was always my home." He pointed to the ruins, and Sue imagined that for him the massive house rose up again each time he came, its roof and walls intact, its doors deep-set, its carved cornices in place.

The picnic party gathered in the shadow of an arch, and everyone helped Pepe set up the chairs and table, arrange the cloth, and extract five glasses from a basket. Into four of these the old man, with remarkable agility, poured red wine. Don Enrique explained the fifth glass. "The padre from the village often joins us. You may meet him."

Bud looked at Sue and shook his head. She saw him think, Another waste of time.

Before seating his guests, Don Enrique proposed a toast. "To the lives we have lived," he said. The others raised their glasses. "And to the one ahead," he continued, and all drank to this immediate simplification of their futures.

Then Don Enrique kicked away an anthill and some thorny stalks and drew out a chair for Sue on his right. Pepe, meanwhile, laid four plates and an earthenware dish on the table.

"Who made these good tacos?" Sue asked, and found that Pepe's elderly daughter was in charge of Don Enrique's kitchen in La Luz.

Bud swallowed a small green chile whole, choked, said, "Jesus," and reached for his wineglass.

Don Enrique pondered his two guests. How can they afford it, he wondered, how pay for this exceptional land? "Now that you see Amapolas again, you are disappointed," he declared in a statement directed mainly at Sue, though it was Bud who responded, in English, "Hell, no."

"I don't expect to change my mind," said Sue. But she had in fact noticed for the first time the depleted look of the earth on which her house would stand, the dangerous drop where the rise fell away at one end above the village and the lake. She had observed the rugged terrain, the absence of trees except for a scattering of scrub oaks. The surrounding hills were lower than she remembered, the cornfields fewer, the distant mountain peak scaled down.

"That is a volcanic cone," said Don Enrique, following her gaze. "What do you think of the lake?"

"It's a little smaller than I remembered it."

"And consider this, señora, it is larger now, and deeper, than it will be next spring during the dry season."

"Do poppies ever grow here?" she asked.

"I think my mother said so. I've never seen them for myself."

Then Pepe brought grapes and cheese and opened another bottle of wine, while Don Enrique, urged on by the old man's nods, began an outline of family history. Sue leaned forward. At the first mention of a sixteenth-century Spanish count, Bud pushed back from the table, upsetting his chair, and before long could be seen at some distance, stepping off great squares.

"On my father's side," Don Enrique went on, "a governor, a conductor of the national symphony, a rector of the university. On my mother's, a foreign minister and two bishops."

The three still at the table sat a moment in silence, warmed by the splendor that radiated from the Ortiz de León genealogies.

"Many of them born in the house that once stood here." Don Enrique waved toward the collapsed pillars and strewn rubble of his ancestors' former bastion and country seat. "There were generals on both sides," he added. "And recognized scholars."

Sue sank without resistance into the past. "And the house," she said. "I suppose it was destroyed in the revolution."

At this, Pepe gathered his waning reserves and rose, joint by joint, to describe the Revolution of 1910, a good deal of which he had witnessed. But his teeth were so few and the images he sought so reluctant to come that of all he said Sue understood only two words, "burn" and "kill."

Don Enrique, middle-aged and childless, listened as though for the first time, until at last Pepe stopped in midsentence and sat down.

Sue glanced behind her at the scattered traces of the former house. "So now there is nothing left."

"One bed," said Don Enrique. But he did not describe this bed—tall-posted and canopied, cradle of illustrious infants—that had by some special grace survived. Nor did he mention it was there, on a hair mattress, that he himself now spent his lengthening nights. He turned his aquiline profile to Sue and looked into the distance, where Bud was tramping back and forth across the land. "What is he doing, the señor Loomis?" he asked. "Is he disoriented?"

"I'm not sure," she said, but it was precisely at this instant—with clouds darkening the day, the plates and glasses still to be packed—that Sue noticed a cold wind from the east and the sudden presence of a stone in her shoe, and finally understood that Bud meant to subdivide the land.

Now Don Enrique was waving in the direction of the village and the lake. Sue watched as first the head, then the shoulders, then all of a black-robed priest came into sight at the edge of the mesa, where a path wound up the bluff. His ascent was so steady and inexorable that even after he was entirely in view it seemed he might rise a few inches more and approach the picnic party with his feet not touching the ground. But he made his way toward them in an ordinary manner, his shoes crushing spiders and ants, his habit collecting nettles.

As he approached, Sue saw that the priest was young—younger than she.

"Here is my friend Padre Miguel," said Don Enrique, and, to the priest, "May I present the señora Susahnah-ahmes? She is one of the new owners and plans to build a house on the spot where we stand."

"Oh, no," Sue said. "Not here. At the far end." She pointed to the place where Padre Miguel had first been seen.

The priest, who saw no difference between the north, south, and center of this strip of land, allowed his gaze to rest on Sue's face. Is this woman a Catholic? he wondered. But he doubted she was.

Of the two or three priests Sue had met in her lifetime, Padre Miguel impressed her as the only one entirely suited to his calling. His eyes burned, and he appeared to have been fasting.

"And here comes Señor Loomis." Don Enrique might have been announcing the players on a soccer team. "He will be joint owner of this land."

Padre Miguel looked into Bud's square, coarse-grained face and believed he saw a troubled man. Two irresolute Americans, thought the priest.

Bud acknowledged the introduction with a nod and pulled Sue to one side. "I've got an idea," he said.

She refused to listen, saying, "Let me tell you where I want my house," and indicating the bluff, beyond which appeared the top of a bell tower, half a church dome, and the outer rim of the lake, which had faded to slate gray under the massing clouds.

Don Enrique overheard. "Not too close to the edge," he warned her. "There's danger of erosion."

"From that point you will look straight down on the cemetery," said the priest in a voice unexpectedly deep for a man his age.

Bud took Sue's arm and propelled her toward the leaning portico of the old house. "This is my idea," he said, and while he spoke of selling lots, Sue studied the volcanic cone, whose sheer sides were faintly green with terraced corn. Eventually, she heard him say, "It's a deal made in heaven." He went on to speak of land as collateral, of cheap labor, of doubling or tripling their money, of a joint reserve in Mexican securities. "These damn bonds pay forty percent," said Bud. "There's no way we can lose. No way."

Sue, pinned against a crumbling pilaster, confronted her own common sense. It's not too late to get out of this, to say my funds are insufficient, my lawyer has strong objections, I'm homesick for Mendocino, California. Then neither of us will have the land, since it's being sold as a single piece and neither of us can pay for it all.

"May I still build my house over there?" She pointed.

"Why not?" said Bud.

Sue turned in a slow circle. The hills, the fields, some stretches of pure desert revolved around her. Far away, a dog barked. A burro, carrying two boys, raised dust on the road to the village. A cow waded into the lake.

And, all at one time, she surrendered her orchard, her vineyard, and half of her view. She said, "All right. Yes."

As soon as they rejoined the others, Padre Miguel invited them to visit the village and the church.

"I've got to get back to the motel," said Bud.

"Next time, Padre," said Don Enrique. "Rain is coming. But have some wine."

When they raised their glasses this time, they simply wished each other health. Pepe, not sure how old he was, drank with relish to this toast and to the years, or perhaps the months, he still had left to live. Soon light rain began to fall. The picnickers and the priest were about to separate when a figure came into sight at the top of the bluff. Skirt flapping, shawl dragging, a little girl ran toward them through the drizzle.

"What now?" said Bud. He gathered up chairs and moved in the direction of the cars.

The barefoot child crossed the stretch of land with astonishing speed. Once arrived, she quickly kissed the padre's ring, then went to Pepe and took his bony hand in hers.

Sue felt a pang, and she began to mourn the child's future in advance. There were never eyes so shadowed as these, never cheeks so scabbed, a neck so stemlike, hair so clotted. When the girl lifted her head to smile at Pepe, she exposed baby and second teeth at odds, competing for space in her mouth.

Don Enrique led her to Sue. "This is Altagracia Gómez," he said. "Pepe's great-granddaughter. After you are settled here, she will come to work for you."

"But she's only a child."

"She is eleven. By the time your house is built, she will be twelve. That is old enough."

How do you know? Sue wanted to ask. Everyone is old enough for something, and too old or young for something else.

A FEW WEEKS later, on another rainy afternoon, the contract was signed in Don Enrique's office under the portrait of his grandmother, a young woman almost too satined, jeweled, ribboned, and combed ever to have lived.

The lawyer had failed to keep his calendar current. The last date checked off was the day before the picnic.

While Don Enrique sorted documents, Bud smoked and crossed and uncrossed his legs.

During this pause, Sue spoke. "I can't believe our good fortune," she said. "This must be the most beautiful piece of land in Mexico."

She's a fool, thought Bud. Any more of this and even now, when we're almost under the wire, she'll drive up the price.

"It's a large property for two people," said Don Enrique. "You will have a pair of ranches."

At this, Bud, abandoning caution, disclosed his project. "Twenty fine lots," he told Don Enrique.

"I thought it was ten," said Sue. Her words were lost in Bud's recital of building plans: street lamps and paved walks, cesspools, and, in time, telephones.

Don Enrique, foolishly neglecting to claim a share of the enterprise, seemed to welcome it anyway. "My godson is an architect," he informed the Americans. "He can help you. His wife may also be of use. She is a weaver, a designer of cloth."

Now each of the three people in the room separately saw a sample house—its individual shape, its *sala* and patio, its textured curtains and hand-loomed spreads. Simultaneously, it occurred to Don Enrique that the town of La Luz was growing too fast, that each day found it noisier and more crowded than the day before. Country air, he began to think, and only a thirty-minute drive from Amapolas to his office. Why not, thought Don Enrique.

There was a knock at the door and Bud started, as if, even here, a federal agent might track him down. But it was only Pepe, trembling under a silver tray, a bottle, and four glasses.

Don Enrique held up his hand. He looked from one to the other of his clients. "Are you Catholics?" he asked, as though he were about to impose a condition of purchase.

"No, why?" asked Bud.

"I used to be an Episcopalian," said Sue.

But Don Enrique had merely been remembering holy days in the village by the lake. He named a few of them. Corpus Christi, Guadalupe, San Juan, Asunción. "These are colorful festivals," he went on. "Perhaps even as Protestants you might wish to see . . ." Here he stopped.

"Oh, yes," said Sue.

Bud had his eye on Pepe and the quivering tray. My God, how old can you get, he wondered.

Then it was done—the agreement signed, the tray set down, the brandy poured, the toast proposed and drunk.

At this moment, in Amapolas del Lago, Altagracia Gómez entered the church to kneel at the back and offer prayers for a necklace and high-heeled shoes.

At the same time, Padre Miguel, on his knees at the altar, prayed to be assigned to another parish, a larger place, where he could be in the company of people who talked well, had talents, examined ideas. Then, for having asked this, he prayed to be forgiven.

AS SOON AS dark came, night animals began to occupy the four *hectáreas* of long flat ground above the village. Each creature followed a purpose of its own—to eat, to mate, to dig a burrow, or simply to run from north to south by moonlight. Heedless of approaching change, they traced the lengths of walls and paths to come. They paused in doorways not yet raised, circled trees not planted. Their footprints webbed the dust of unmarked building sites.

Three gophers, meeting on Sue Ames's plot of land, anticipated her rows of lettuce, beans, and corn, and began to tunnel underground. Slow workers in the dark, they would not find her roses until May.

Easter
Weekend

....

COINCIDENCE IS EVERYTHING. If Susanna Ames had not turned back to remind her watchman to water a tree, she might not have been intercepted by Bud Loomis and they might not have quarreled about the land they owned. Then the shining prospect of her Easter weekend would never have been blighted by a promise.

But Bud, his truck churning dust as it crossed the mesa, caught her as she started the motor of her car. She had to get out.

Her business partner was staring at her new adobe house, of which part of the floor, all of the windowpanes, and the front door were missing.

"I'm leaving early tomorrow to spend the weekend in Santa Prisca," Sue said in an effort to cut short any dialogue between them.

But Bud had no interest in the colonial towns of Mexico or in the saints who protected them. He gazed silently at Sue's house, which overlooked the village and the shallow lake of Amapolas. The windows that had no glass framed uncounted miles of view to the north and east.

"You can see the whole damn place from here," he remarked without interest. His eyes fell on a youth, all bones and joints, slouched across the empty threshold.

"Who's the kid?" asked Bud.

"It's my watchman, Patricio Gómez," Sue told him, in the same tone of respect in which she might have said, "It's Janus, god of doorways and beginnings."

"Can he handle a gun?" Bud asked, and shook his head without waiting for an answer.

Turning from the unseen eastern panorama to assess the flat mesa to the west, he pointed a blunt finger in the direction of Don Enrique's crumbling *hacienda*, then gestured with his thumb toward Sue's whitewashed house behind him.

"So far, these two are all we've got," he said. "And that one's got to go." He indicated the falling ruins.

Sue's eyes followed his, but instead of projecting building sites, saw only space, silence, and an extended calm interval of time. She glanced at Bud's flat profile and thought, I was out of my mind to go into business with this man.

Bud spoke again. He said, "We need dough," and went on to explain that grading the land, even though he hired local farmers at bottom wage, had run more than he figured. The bank was stalling on a second loan. He kicked a pile of adobe bricks and talked of pumps, wells, transformers, and a tractor.

"Take a look at that," he said, his aggravated stare on the ravaged *hacienda*. "No one's going to haul it off for nothing."

Sue, surveying the massive walls, believed she saw fragments of carved stone fall to the ground as she watched. Don Enrique's ancestral seat, with its fluted columns and wreathed balustrades, slanted earthward as if drawn to final repose.

She drew a breath to stiffen her courage.

"Let's leave it where it is," she said. "Strewn about," and Bud turned to face her, temporarily speechless.

Sue watched his face redden. Having gone so far, she went further.

"Let's give it back to Don Enrique," she said. "The walls that are left, and the stone fragments, and the land they're on."

"You're talking about a full acre," Bud managed to say, and before the absorbed gaze of Patricio Gómez, they argued.

Patricio, comfortable and silent in the doorway, listened

without comprehension to the dispute that followed. The young North American señora allowed her voice to rise and the North American señor, who was known in the village as El Chaparro because he was short, paced back and forth and shouted. The quarrel was so intense that at times Patricio expected the señor to strike the señora, as many men in Amapolas, under the same circumstances, might have struck their women. Then all at once the señora lifted a calm hand as though she had divine power and spoke the necessary words. As suddenly as it began, the argument ended, and the two, without exchanging another word, drove off, she in her yellow *camioneta* and he in his dusty pickup.

This much Patricio saw. Later, in the village, he would say, "The young señora has rejected the señor. She is beautiful and he is . . . well, you have seen him."

But Sue, in fact, had ended the controversy with a promise. She told Bud that, if he agreed to let Don Enrique keep the *hacienda*, she would sell one of the empty lots this weekend in Santa Prisca.

"Is that a promise?"

Sue said, "You have my word."

ALL THIS WAS yesterday.

At eight o'clock today, while Sue ate breakfast in the Posada del Sol, Bud entered the dining room in haste, mistakenly ordering coffee from a dark-suited guest who happened to be standing in the doorway.

He joined Sue at her table near the window and she knew at once his mood had changed.

"I went ahead and saw the old guy last night," Bud said, adding a few decades to the age of the forty-five-year-old lawyer. "I worked out a deal with him."

Sue, forcing herself to imagine she was alone, broke her roll and gazed through the window at the plaza of La Luz. Under the Indian laurels, which were in new green leaf, children and dogs circled the benches and ran back to circle them again.

"Get a load of this," said Bud.

It appeared that Don Enrique in his gratitude had offered not only to set what remained of the *hacienda* in order, but to arrange a number of conveniences that would benefit the developers. "You and the señora Susahnahahmes," Don Enrique had said.

As it turned out, Don Enrique César Ortiz de León was a first cousin of the director of the water department in La Luz. The manager of light and power was his sister's widower. Don Enrique owned a stony piece of land that had a spring on it half a kilometer from the hill at Amapolas. He had gone to school with the governor of the state.

"All we need now is cash," Bud said. He winked at Sue and left.

Half an hour later she was on the point of leaving, stand-ing at the reception desk, her suitcase at her feet, when all at once, filling the entrance with his lean height, Don En-rique appeared.

He approached Sue, bowed over her hand, and, in front of the manager and the hotel *mozo*, boy of all jobs, began to thank her for the gift of his forefathers' birthplace. The fact that there remained only the ghost of a structure, supported almost entirely by the force of his memory, failed to dimin-ish his happiness. It was clear to Sue that, if he could, Don Enrique would at this moment have summoned his dead forebears from their graves to surround her where she stood and shower upon her their spectral expressions of delight.

Sue repeated, "It is nothing," until at last she lifted her suitcase and took a step toward the door. She said, "If I don't leave now, I'll arrive in Santa Prisca after dark."

Don Enrique took the suitcase from her hand and the *mozo* took it from his.

"Easter is dangerous for travelers," said the lawyer. "There are more deaths on the highways during Holy Week than at any other time." He regarded with concern Sue's distracted gaze and the strands of light hair that flew out from her face.

"Besides the congestion of traffic," he went on, "reli-gious pilgrims crowd the edges of the pavement." He saw that Sue was backing toward the door and only added, "I wish you a safe arrival and a safe return," and pulled open the door.

The manager and the *mozo* nodded and together the three men watched her circle the plaza and drive away.

A L L   O F   I T was true. There were too many trucks and too many cars, and too much dust and too hot a sun. Straggling bands of pilgrims ventured onto the pavement. Each time she passed these penitents she glanced left and right to find what distant altars were their goal, but there was never a church in sight.

She had driven no more than an hour when she began to regret her trip, dread the four days, no longer carefree, in Santa Prisca. As distance shrank before her and accumulated behind, she started to scan passing cars in search of a likely buyer of real estate at Amapolas. But even if she had singled someone out, it would have proved impossible to flag the prospect down on this thoroughfare that wound up mountains and unrolled through valleys, that rose and sank through temperature zones from mountain peaks to desert floor.

At two o'clock she ate a sandwich in a high meadow bordered by pines. An hour later she was peeling an orange in hot country. It was here she consulted her guidebook to calculate the remaining kilometers to Santa Prisca.

There is still time to arrive by daylight, Sue assured

herself a moment later, and turned back to the highway.

An hour further into this parched, unpromising landscape Sue started to look for a gas station. Eventually she had to ask help from a band of pilgrims resting in the thin shade of a mesquite tree. Several responded, "Ten kilometers," and pointed.

Following instructions, she left the highway at a sign whose single arrow was directed toward two settlements, Seco and El Polvo. And when she passed the dozen dwellings and shriveled vegetation of the place called Dry, she saw no other name would have suited it, and when she arrived in the larger settlement of Dust she realized that was what it had to be called.

Finding without difficulty the single pump that faced the wilting plaza, she remained in her car, sealed from the whirling grit that, as she watched, began to scar her windshield. After no more than a moment the attendant, who was also the manager and owner of the station, tapped on her window.

She lowered it an inch and spoke. "Is the tank full?"

"Half full," he said. "But that is all the gasoline I have."

"Is it enough to take me to Santa Prisca?"

"Of course. Why not?" said the dusty man.

IN THE END it was still dusk when she reached Santa Prisca. The first of the inadequate street lamps came on as she shifted into low gear on the hill and made her careful way past the church and around a plaza dense with children, dogs, beggars, pilgrims, and sightseers.

Then she climbed an even steeper, narrower street in a confusion of burros, carts, pedestrians, and a bus, and at the top encountered the realization of a dream. For so the Hotel Miranda appeared to her, made up as it was of quantities of flowers in baskets and pots, the music of two guitars, a terrace of dinner tables lit by candles, and, lifted from the square below, the audible murmur of the crowd.

Chava, the desk clerk, looked up as this lovely woman opened her mouth, exposed perfect teeth, and in the accents of a learner of the language said she had reserved a room. He handed her the pen as if it were an exotic bloom.

She wrote her name on the form, and the clerk, like Don Enrique César Ortiz de León before him, pronounced it to himself. She is Susahnahahmes, he privately recorded. Engaged as he was in examining her bent head and thick lashes, it was not until she had printed her address and license number that he turned to consult his chart of rooms.

Stricken, he faced her. "*Ay*, señorita, there has been a mistake." His voice mourned the error. "Your reservation is for a week from today." Regarding her with compassion, he added, "And all our rooms are taken."

"But I must have a room," Sue insisted, driven by her promise to Bud. "I have important business in Santa

Prisca." She turned to glance at the diners on the terrace, perhaps expecting one of them to rise, enter the lobby, and ask, "Do you know of a piece of land for sale near a lake three hundred miles north of here?"

Chava was speaking. "There is no room to rent in all of Santa Prisca," he told her, speaking quietly because of his broken heart. When she said nothing, he went on. "Things are not normal here. It is Holy Week."

Silence fell, and a pall that was almost visible descended to shroud the clerk and Susanna Ames at the reception desk. Into it, from a chair in the corner, stepped a woman.

"You can have my room," this person said to Sue in English. "It's more than I need. I can move in with a friend." In quick Spanish she instructed the clerk to call the *mozo*, call the maid, transfer the luggage, prepare the room.

Before Sue could protest, Chava had tapped his bell for service.

"I really can't accept," she tried to say, but this woman, older than Sue, tall and narrow, black haired and quick eyed, was already at the street entrance. She disappeared into the evening with a single wave of her hand.

"The señora Bowles," Chava said, as if to clarify the turn of events. Then he showed Sue to a chair, said, "Allow me a moment," and returned with a daiquiri from the bar. From behind his desk he watched Sue drink it.

She detected within herself an erosion of self-assurance,

a weakening of resolve. In order to reestablish authority, she addressed the clerk in a formal tone.

"I will have breakfast in my room at eight," she said. "Orange juice, coffee, and a roll." Then she added in a stern voice, "It must be brought on time. I have an urgent matter to attend to in the morning."

Chava, twenty-seven years old, married, and the father of five, listened entranced to the señorita's precise, slow words. He noticed her eyes were green, like wet bay leaves.

THE NEXT MORNING, after nine hours of obliterating sleep, Sue stepped out of her shuttered room into a landscape so bright she raised a hand to shield her eyes.

A war of colors raged from her balcony down the steep length of the road, across the plaza, and, in a final siege, up to the massive doors of the church. The housefronts that lined the way had been painted in all the shades of fruit from lemon yellow to plum purple to watermelon red. Vendors spilled rainbows of scarves and shawls onto the ground. Riotous vines, heavy with blossoms, flung themselves from eaves to balustrades to garden paths. Sue leaned over the parapet to look down on a sheer rock wall, its cracks laced with ferns.

From here she saw balconies adjoining her own and others beyond them, each one hanging over Santa Prisca. On the low brick barriers between them, massed pots of geraniums rose like flowering walls.

Sue sat on a leather chair at a round leather-topped table and sank without resistance into layers of light. She had almost achieved euphoria when her breakfast tray arrived, carried by the waiter, with the desk clerk at his heels.

There followed an inspection of the orange juice, coffee, and roll. Sue discovered a spray of honeysuckle next to her cup, lifted it, and said, "Thank you." Now one of them is going to unfold the napkin and spread it across my knees, she supposed, but the two men appeared to have taken root where they stood.

Sue had to bring herself to say, like a queen, "That will be all," before they would turn on their heels and leave. Then for a moment or two she allowed herself simply to exist.

She had barely lifted the pot to pour her coffee when she heard voices on the next balcony. A woman's voice and a man's voice. They laughed. They put cups down on plates. They dropped a spoon. Sue tried to eliminate them by force of will, but there they remained, a few feet away, two obviously happy people.

Now a woman's head appeared over the geraniums. It was the señora Bowles, who had given up her room last night and moved in with a friend.

"How did you sleep?" she said and, without waiting for

an answer, called, "Paco." The head of a smiling, red-haired man promptly appeared next to hers above the intervening flowers.

"I'm Frances Bowles," said the woman, "and this is Francisco Alvarado." Then both waited for Sue's name.

"Susanna Ames," she said, and for a brief moment lost herself in contemplation. They have the same name, she reflected. They are Francisco and Francisca. Does that make them more suited to each other? she wondered. And suddenly, for no reason, she remembered in astonishing detail the eyes, hands, and voice of the husband she had left. If her name had been Jane and his John, if they had been Juan and Juana, would they still be together?

Sue extended her hand to her new acquaintances. Then, as though she were expected to make an announcement, said, "I'm divorced."

After a short pause, Frances Bowles said, "Have lunch with me. Paco will be out of town on business."

Business, thought Sue, and remembered her own. Perhaps I should start with these people.

THE TWO WOMEN ate lunch under a fringed white cotton umbrella and soon had shortened their names to Fran and Sue. Below them a mass of pilgrims, townspeople, and visitors, swaying vans and buses, together with animals bent on suicide, overflowed the precipitous street and were being swept, as if by gravity, into the plaza. All at once, above the commotion, the church bell, tolling the quarter hour, rang out with a sound as clear as rain.

"That bell must have silver in it," Sue said, and her new friend nodded.

Fran then went on to reveal much of her personal history. Starting with Paco Alvarado, she unwound her life backward until she reached her childhood in Santa Fe, New Mexico.

Sue marveled at Fran's willingness to expose herself. She spoke of Paco (twice a widower), of his children (three by each wife), of his two mothers-in-law (with each of whom the appropriate grandchildren lived). With one family in Puebla and the other in Toluca and his Mexico City apartment in the middle, he was a pendulum that swung from east to west between them.

Fran also had married twice. "Grave errors," she said of these unions. "I'll never marry again." She paused and added, "Though I'm fond of Paco. Very fond." A shadow clouded her face and settled behind her eyes. She had the look of a sailor who had set out in a listing boat in spite of storm warnings.

"I'm here on business," she went on in a matter-of-fact tone, as if in this manner she could gain control of her uncertain craft. "So is Paco."

Sue was about to say, "And so am I," when their waiter, the same one who had brought her breakfast earlier, appeared at their table to slap his napkin at a fly, brush away crumbs, and observe her at close range.

"The bill, please," Fran Bowles said, and in the calm that followed told Sue she was writing a book on Mexico. "A travel book of sorts," she said, and added that she had a contract with a publisher.

Before Sue could ask how long she had lived in this country, how well she knew the people, had she seen it all, Fran looked at her watch, initialed the bill, hung a pumpkin-colored straw bag over her shoulder, and vanished. A few minutes later, Sue, gazing down into the crowd, saw her join a man with a camera. Then they were swept away.

Sue spent the afternoon on her balcony with her sketchbook and crayons, calculating the space between the town and the ring of hills, sorting out roofs and alleys, measuring towers and domes, crowding in the bougainvillea and the climbing rose, deranged by color, giddy with light, working until dark came on.

WAKING AT MIDNIGHT to the silver clang of the church bell, she left her bed and followed a strip of moonlight to her balcony, where the table, chairs, and flowerpots, now turned pale and weightless, floated in the radiant air. Lifted by the magic of the night, she might have floated too, had not low voices speaking an occasional word issued from the adjoining room. Unaccustomed as she had lately been to being loved in bed or out, she nevertheless recognized at once the intensity of the fondness Fran Bowles had spoken of at lunch. Hurriedly removing herself as a witness, Sue returned to her room, closed the balcony door, and lay in the dark across her bed, from which she continued to hear through the wall Spanish words of love she had not known existed.

She pulled two pillows over her ears and was on the verge of sleep when the image of her former husband, Tim, fully dressed and laughing, rose up to stand at the foot of her bed.

A DRIVE INTO the country on Good Friday had not been Sue's intention. Her plan was to witness the procession of penitents and follow them to the religious service.

"To observe the *penitentes* on Holy Friday in Santa Prisca," Don Enrique had told her one afternoon in Amapolas, "is to see into the heart of the Catholic faith."

It would be impossible to explain to him why she had missed it, as impossible as it would have been to explain her attendance to Bud Loomis.

But there had been no denying Fran and Paco, whose heads had again appeared over the flowers at breakfast. They wanted to take Sue for a drive in the country.

"I want to show you a waterfall," Paco said in excellent English, one of the results, Sue was to learn, of his two years at Harvard.

An hour later they were on the road.

"We are lucky to be out of town today," Fran said, lowering the window a few inches to let old dust out and new dust in.

The day was hot and the drive longer than anticipated, even by Paco. An hour out of Santa Prisca he turned off the road at a charred tree stump and onto a lane rutted by cart wheels.

Fran, sitting in front with him, said, "Is this the best way?" and Paco explained it was a shortcut. A second hour passed as the car wound its way around hills and through gullies, sometimes losing the dirt track completely and having to proceed cross-country between spiked branches of cactus and over broken stones. During this time neither woman spoke.

Sue silently noticed the presence in this landscape, so far from the voting booth, of the initials ALM painted on boulders and an occasional tree trunk. Staring out at the chipped, streaked letters, she remembered that Adolfo López Mateos had already been president of Mexico for five years.

Eventually, the car ceased its drifting and rejoined the road it had left not far from the point where it had left it.

"Oh, do forget the waterfall," Fran said crossly to Paco. "All I can think of is cold lemonade."

At this, Paco reversed the car's direction without a word and headed back to Santa Prisca. This behavior, almost docile, surprised Sue, who had already classified him as a headstrong man, not short on self-esteem.

Twenty minutes later, on a lane bordered by willows, a billboard appeared on the right. SQUEEZE, it advertised in brilliant letters, then told the passerby how to say it. PRO-NÚNCIESE "ESCUIS," it suggested. Beyond the curve, Paco slowed at a hand-painted sign, REFRESCOS, and stopped a moment later in the dooryard of a farm.

"Lemonade," Paco announced to his passengers, and blew his horn for service. Then, offering the women a second or two of his brilliant smile, he seated them at a table facing each other across a length of oilcloth scarred with bottle rings, the more recent of which were attracting flies.

The farmer's wife now appeared from inside the house, closing behind her a massive door, its wood rich with age, dark with history.

"Lemonade for three," Paco ordered, and the woman said, "All I can offer you is Pepsi and Escuis."

When the bottles were brought, the three visitors drank the sweet contents in silence. The air was heavy with sunlight and the smell of goats in a nearby corral. Sue, about to fall asleep, rose to examine the plants the farmer's wife had chosen to border the front of her house.

At this evidence of interest, the woman appeared again and began to point and give names.

"Calla lily," she said, then, "begonia," indicating a plant in an oil can and then one in a tin labeled KEROSENE. She pointed to a nasturtium in a rusty chamberpot and a rose in a gasoline drum.

"And what is this?" Sue asked, touching a cactus whose red-flowered thorny branches had been staked and wired to form a circle. Paco, appearing suddenly behind Sue, said, "It's called a crown of thorns," and added, "very appropriate to today."

The farmer's wife was cutting a length from another branch. "Like this, señora," she said. "As soon as you plant one end, start to shape the crown at the other. But cautiously. Wear gloves." And she wrapped the spiked branch in newspaper and laid it on the back seat of the car.

Once back on the road, Sue remarked, "That old door. I wish I could find one like it."

"What for?" asked Fran, who had presumed her new acquaintance to be a tourist, in Mexico for a short visit.

"Have you heard of a village called Amapolas? On the edge of a lake?" Sue asked. Then suddenly the car slowed for a procession of pilgrims, and the church towers of Santa Prisca were in sight.

At the Hotel Miranda, Sue transferred the cutting into the soft soil of one of the potted geraniums on her balcony. It was easy to convince herself, standing over the celebrants and onlookers still crowding the plaza below, that future occupants of her room would concern themselves with the training of the branch. Sue had already tied a length of cord to the tip, bent it slightly, and secured it at its base. All that future guests in these quarters needed to do was gradually tighten the cord and allow time to pass.

ON SATURDAY, THE two women walked into the sun-struck morning and made their way down to the plaza and to the shop of a man who sold doors. The hillside bore witness to yesterday's crowds. Litter of all sorts, from fruit rinds to glass shards to the droppings of animals, lay between the cobblestones. Weekend visitors, their penance behind them, thronged around the outdoor displays of baskets, sandals, hats, and shawls. In groups and separately, the devout pushed their way through the courtyard in front of the church. At the baroque stone fountain an old man and three dogs were drinking out of the greenish bowl.

Now, for the first time, Sue and Fran became aware of the presence of a horde of beggars.

Fran Bowles said, "Most of them come from other towns. They travel great distances by bus to be here during Holy Week."

Each woman emptied her purse of coins. The response from the supplicants never varied. One after another, they said, "May God repay you," and the two women, acknowledging this vast promise, said, "Thanks."

The man who sold doors lived on a terraced slope just

beyond the bell tower's shadow. His house clung to the top, below it a corral for a goat and a pig, and still lower a rambling structure that slanted toward the bottom of the hill. This person, ancient, seamed, and toothless, led the way to the windowless shed and, once inside, lit a single bulb that hung from the roof. In this faint light Sue saw she had entered a treasure house of doors and shutters, all old, all works of art, propped six deep against streaked adobe walls.

While Fran Bowles waited, Sue touched wood, took measurements, and finally chose.

"This one," she said. "Look at the hinges. Look at the lock."

"That door used to be at the entrance to the jail," said the owner. "Who can count the unfortunates who heard it close behind them?"

"I'll take it," Sue said.

"Will you want shutters also?" asked the old man. He pulled one forward. "This is one of a group. They were once at the windows of a house of assignation in the town."

Sue noted their proportions. She touched the wood. "Yes. Those, too."

She signed papers while Fran looked on.

"Everything is to be shipped here," Sue told the aged man, "to Amapolas by way of La Luz," and, as she spoke, was assailed once again by an image of the mesa above the lake, and of its vacant plots of land, and of her promise.

....

LATER SHE SAT on her balcony, drinking lemonade with Fran Bowles.

"I've never heard of La Luz or Amapolas," said Fran.

Sue told her that La Luz occasionally appeared on maps,
Amapolas never. Her unfinished adobe house was above the
town, she said, on a long flat rise known as Lomas de Amapolas or, as her business partner called it, Poppy Heights.
She was about to describe the view when Fran broke in.

"What partner?" she said, and Sue, for the first of what
would later prove to be a number of times, found herself
explaining Bud.

"Bud Loomis," she said and, bit by bit, explained to
Fran how she had driven from California to Mexico and
by chance discovered La Luz, then Amapolas. All of it
happened by chance, Sue said, nothing by plan. No one
would plan to meet Bud Loomis, she told Fran, or to
dismember an important piece of land.

"Are you selling lots?" asked Fran, and Sue quickly said,
"Do you or Paco have a friend who wants a country place?"

Fran ignored this question, but within half an hour she
knew that Don Enrique's *hacienda* lay half-scattered on
the ground, that Patricio Gómez, fifteen years old and
stationed in the doorway, was all that stood between Sue's
incomplete house and its ruin, that four brightly painted

houses on the shore were reflected every evening in the lake. She heard about the air and the view, about the water pipes and powerlines to be installed, and the eventual telephone.

Fran Bowles listened, looked at her watch, and said, as if it naturally followed, "I believe I am becoming an embarrassment to Paco." She picked up her bright orange bag and left.

Sue spent the afternoon sketching on her balcony. Turning her back on Santa Prisca, she crayoned a series of recollections. She filled one page with a country chapel. She drew the main street of the town called Seco and the gas station in El Polvo. In the waning light, she outlined a penitent, a beggar, and a priest.

Fran, appearing without warning, spoke from the next balcony.

"What's all that?" she said, and reached over the screen of flowers.

Sue handed her one page and then another until Fran had seen them all.

Fran said, "Are these for sale?" and then, as though it were part of the same conversation, went on, "I may buy one of your lots. One or two."

BUT "MAY BUY" is not the same as "will buy," and on Easter morning Sue advised Chava, pensive behind the desk, that she might require her room for another day or two.

The clerk consulted his chart. "It is yours for a week," he said. "Perhaps longer," and he saw at once by the eyes of this Susahnahahmes that she was tempted.

But she said, "Oh no, not that long. Surely I will find someone before then."

Chava, longing to offer himself for whatever the endeavor might be, said only, "*A sus órdenes.*"

AT NINE O'CLOCK that evening, Sue had brandy with Fran and Paco at the edge of the terrace that hung like an observation platform over Santa Prisca. Behind them, although most of the diners had gone, candles still burned on the tables.

"*Salud,*" the three said to each other and raised their glasses. Then no one talked until Fran said, "We've decided." She addressed Sue, but her eyes were on Paco. "A house on your hill is what we must have," and again Sue recognized in Fran's voice the fondness she had heard through her bedroom wall.

Paco explained his position. He said, "The two families of children, the two grandmothers, my apartment halfway between . . ." He paused and said, "Ah, Francisca," and lifted his glass to her. Then he lifted it to Sue and said, "My second and happiest home will be at your lake."

She looked down on the scattered streetlights of the town

and on the facade of the church, still brilliantly illuminated to mark the day.

At last she said, "So you will buy a lot," not sure whether to address Fran or Paco.

It was Fran who spoke. "I'll buy one," she said, "on condition that everything you've told me is true." She laughed and Paco smiled.

After a moment's silence, Fran spoke again. "And then there's my mother," she said.

Sue stared. Until now, Fran had impressed her as motherless, someone who had no living parents and only a remote connection with them in the past.

"Mother will buy her own lot," said Fran.

Sue heard herself ask, "How old is she?"

"Almost eighty," Fran said. "She lived in Mexico as a child and wants to die here."

As though Bud Loomis had materialized out of the night, Sue clearly perceived his stocky frame and listened to his uncomplicated speech.

"We don't want to turn the place into a damn Sunset City," Bud said.

IN THIS WAY, the future of the mesa was assured. The *hacienda* would stand again, its back to the hill, its restored facade confronting the newly built houses of aliens. It was here, in its shadow, that Sue intended to spend the rest of her life.

Goya and
the Widow
Bowles

....

In late summer, Ursula Bowles, accompanied by a drumroll of thunder, lightning, and drenching rain, arrived in the Mexican village where she expected, sooner or later, to die. Here, on a bluff above the town of Amapolas, she had bought a house, sight unseen. Today was her seventy-ninth birthday.

Her taxi driver and a local youth, who had appeared out of empty space, were carrying in her luggage when she stopped them.

"Please wait," she said in Spanish, then repeated the words, "*Esperen, por favor*," remembering that the single verb meant both to wait and hope. This extraordinary language, she thought.

45

And, with the two men restless behind her, she crossed the bare floor of her *sala* to a window and began to name the things she saw.

"*El panteón*," she said, looking down on an overgrown graveyard where a ragbag of a woman was pulling a goat through the rows of tilting crosses.

"*La iglesia*," pronounced Ursula Bowles, noting that the church had only a small purple dome and a carved bell tower to recommend it.

"*El lago.*" Now she sounded pleased, for the rains had deepened the lake of Amapolas and stretched its surface enough to reflect a streamer of sunlight that had burst through the clouds from the west.

Ursula went on to indicate cornfields, a vineyard, a flooded arroyo and, returning her gaze to the scene below, remarked, "An old woman is allowing her goat to graze in the *campo santo*."

While the taxi driver and the youth, who had introduced himself as Patricio Gómez, listened in silence, the elderly newcomer remarked that she had been born in a town only half a day's drive from here and that now she would make Amapolas her home for as long as she lived.

That could be any moment from tomorrow to the end of the next decade, thought Patricio. Some people live a long time. His great-grandfather, already grown when Pancho Villa shot his way through here in 1910, could still walk a flat mile. The fact that this aged *Norteamericana* could communicate in Spanish disappointed Patricio. With the coming of these people who know the language, we are losing our liberty to speak, he remarked to himself.

The taxi driver, finally paid, started away so fast that his rear wheels spun in the mud until bricks were wedged under them. Ursula, standing in the doorway of her new house, watched him until he disappeared, heading south toward the city of La Luz, and his wife, and their supper of sweet rolls, and the wide matrimonial bed that, she supposed, half filled their small apartment.

"Permit me, señora," Patricio said, and, as though he could see the contents, carried suitcases to the bedroom, boxes to the hall, paper bags to the kitchen, and a twist of newspaper that held geranium cuttings to a corner of the garden. He lit two lamps, opened a bottle of drinking water, then hesitated at the door.

Should this old person be left alone? Where was her daughter, Francisca, whose unfinished house next door dripped windowless in the rain? Or the person in charge of these houses, where was she, the señora Sue?

At that, as though Patricio's concern had summoned her, here she was, Susanna Ames, apologizing, explaining, closing curtains, opening drawers, setting a match to the kindling on the hearth and under the kettle on the stove.

"Exactly where is Frances?" Ursula asked, and Sue, forced to answer, said, "I'm not quite sure."

THAT NIGHT AT ten o'clock, Ursula Bowles, recent widow, mother of one, longtime object of a man's whole love, almost but not quite ready to die, stepped out of her house into the starry night.

She smelled wet leaves, wet earth, jasmine, animal dung, smoke from a charcoal fire. She heard the church bell strike, a man shout, a woman laugh. A night bird sang two notes. A burro brayed.

Speaking aloud, she addressed the dark.

"I was right to come," she said. "Yes."

FROM THE FIRST, Ursula was known to the people of Amapolas as the widow Bowles.

"The widow Bowles has dresses of every color except black," said a woman washing clothes at the lake's edge.

"She pours wine and lights candles every night, even when she eats alone," said another.

"She talks to herself," said a third, "as though there were someone else in the house."

Not far back from the shore, a very old woman sat in the shade of a cottonwood tree. This was Gregoria Ramos, of vast but uncertain age, assumed in the village to be deaf, dumb, and nearly blind. A white film clouded her eyes and

rags stuffed her ears against the cold. The people of Amapolas called her Goya.

Here this Goya sat, apart from the other women, taking
no more notice of them than they of her. Attached to her
by a length of rope tied around her waist, a goat foraged
nearby on nettles and discarded watermelon rind.

URSULA BOWLES SLEPT late the day after her
arrival and only in the brilliant light of midmorning discovered a card from her daughter Frances under a kerosene
lamp.

"Welcome!" wrote Fran Bowles. "Happy 79th! I wanted
to celebrate with you, but something came up." She went
on to explain that Paco, a man she'd been seeing a lot, was
unexpectedly free for a week and the two of them had gone
to Guanajuato. "We have so little time together," wrote
the widow's daughter. "I'm sure you understand. If not
now, you will when you meet him. Be as happy with your
house as Paco and I will be with mine. Love, Frances."
There was a scribbled postscript. Sue Ames and Patricio
would look in every day. Altagracia Gómez would come
to clean.

And before the widow could adjust to the fact of Paco
standing and lying at her daughter's side, here was Altagracia at the door, bringing a basket of eggs and a napkin
folded over hot tortillas.

"Good morning," said the aproned child, and she entered the room to examine the widow's things.

This Altagracia, shy, awkward, and not yet into her teens, might still grow into beauty, Ursula observed, noticing the girl's fine bones, intense eyes, and even brows. Her hair was smoothly pulled back into braids, her bare feet buckled into sandals. The widow noticed something noble and familiar about her profile.

"Are you related to Patricio?" she asked.

"My brother," Altagracia said, and broke into a smile so wide that all of her teeth were exposed, each one wrapped in metal and wired to the next. As if the widow might have missed an eyetooth or a molar, Altagracia opened her mouth even wider and pointed.

"The señora Sue takes me," she said. "Today will be the fourth time."

"Does it hurt?" asked Ursula, for such a rearrangement must necessarily bring pain, but Altagracia shook her head and fell silent.

She could have told the elderly American that the weekly trips to La Luz were her chief joys and the hours in the tilting chair the high points of her existence. She enjoyed spitting into the swirling water at her side and looking into the dentist's cocoa brown eyes so close to hers.

Altagracia could also have told the widow that once, many months ago, on the first day she came to work, the señora Sue had bathed her in her own tub and after that taken her to a *salón* in La Luz. Here one specialist had shampooed and cut and combed her hair while another trimmed the nails of her toes and fingers.

But she only said, "My next appointment with the dentist is in one hour," and hurried off down the muddy road.

Bud Loomis, Sue Ames's partner in land development, called on Ursula Bowles soon after that, in order to discuss an assessment for the water system.

At the moment the widow opened her door, Sue Ames could be seen two houses away, driving off in her car with Altagracia Gómez on the seat beside her.

"Where the hell are they going?" said Bud, unaware of his associate's latest folly.

EVEN BEFORE HER daughter could introduce her, Ursula Bowles began to receive callers. These included the village mayor, who owned its only restaurant, and the schoolmaster, who looked school age himself. On two occasions, Don Enrique Ortiz de León came with fragments of carved stone for her garden. The widow was much taken with these gifts. She placed a cracked panel twined with grapevine beside the now-rooted geraniums and a crumbling cherub's foot at one end of a row of lettuce.

Besides these dignitaries, a number of curious children and their aunts and mothers climbed the steep path up the bluff to meet this newest North American and discover, if they could, why she was here on this barren rise over-looking Amapolas, a town of unpaved streets that still lacked drains. At the end of an hour these visitors would slip and slide down the bluff, no wiser than when they had come.

Even the young priest called and left confounded. The widow had poured two cups of tea, led him to the terrace under the gathering clouds of late afternoon, and asked about inoculations and nutrition.

"We expect a government intern within the next few months," Padre Miguel informed her.

"Is there a park with swings and slides?" she asked, and was told the leveling of the soccer field just beyond the cemetery must come first. And Ursula, leaning over the low wall that marked the brink of the cliff, could see for herself the need was great, for cows grazed among the puddles on the soccer field and two burros were tethered there. She gazed briefly at the cemetery, where fresh-picked flowers brightened a mound.

The priest's glance followed hers.

"Does the proximity of the *panteón* sadden you?" he asked.

"Oh, no," said the widow, who in New Mexico not long ago had deposited her husband's ashes, as he had requested, on a windy slope of the Sangre de Cristo range. She contemplated the cemetery.

"I may go down there with some wildflower seeds," she said.

Another heretic on the hill, thought Padre Miguel, and this one in her final years, and so far fearless.

IN THE WEEK before her daughter's return from her trip, the widow received one visitor three times. This was the ancient Goya, who, dragging her goat behind her, entered Ursula's gate without a word and in silence shuffled to a bench on the terrace.

"Good afternoon," the widow said each time. "Will you have a *refresco*?" And she passed soft drinks and cookies to the shawled, bent old woman, whose gnarled hand shot out from her layers of garments as quick as a garter snake to accept what was offered.

"Have you always lived in Amapolas?" Ursula had asked on the first occasion, and Goya rose to point out a blue house no bigger than a lean-to on the upper shore of the lake.

"And you have children and grandchildren," the hostess continued, at which Goya nodded in the direction of the graveyard.

The goat, meanwhile, wandered the full length of its rope to explore the widow's garden.

"No, no!" called Ursula when the animal threatened her

single spray of honeysuckle, and Goya, drawing from an unexpected reserve of strength, pulled her four-footed charge sharply back.

So it became plain to the widow Bowles that Goya could see and hear.

After the aged woman's second visit, Ursula questioned Patricio, who was chopping firewood at the kitchen door.

"What happened to Goya's family?" she asked, and a lengthy explanation followed, in which desertion, murder, fatal illness, and ordinary bad luck played important parts.

"Now she is alone," said Patricio.

"WHO IS THAT old woman with the goat?" Fran Bowles asked when she returned tanned and joyous, her hair a smoother black, her eyes a clearer blue, from her week with Paco. But her attention wandered while her mother talked. All the widow's daughter wanted was to have the mason and carpenter out of her house and Paco in it, contented and amused on her sofa, at her table, in her bed.

From her mother's terrace, Fran surveyed the unfinished structure next door. Why, it's quite handsome, she noticed in some surprise, for the house had been built in her absence, as had her mother's. Fran saw that Sue Ames and the architect had performed two miracles out of adobe bricks, mortar, and tiles.

"Did you ever expect such happiness to be simply handed to you?" she asked her mother, who, after allowing segments of her past to flash briefly by, simply said, "Yes."

But she observed that Frances, her parents' long-awaited offspring, looked twenty-five instead of thirty-eight.

"You will love Paco," the widow's daughter said, and was off to Sue's house and the extra bedroom set aside for her until her own, curtained and pillowed by then, could receive the man for whom it was designed.

Ursula's gaze followed her twice–unhappily married and twice-divorced child. She counted the years of her own marriage. Fifty-five.

"Love," she repeated out loud, and at that moment could scarcely have defined it.

ONE SEPTEMBER AFTERNOON, after a visit from Goya and her animal, Ursula talked to Patricio when he came to fill her lamps.

"That goat," the widow said. "Why is it always with her?"

"It is like this, señora," and Patricio lined the lamps up on the kitchen table. "When her last grandchild was left alone, Goya brought him to live with her. He was eight years old and cried for his mother, so one day she gave him a goat."

This is the moment for me to stop this story, Ursula warned herself. It is bound to be disturbing. But she continued to listen while Patricio, in as few words as possible, told her what had happened to Goya.

He said that at first the goat was the color of caramel, and small and sleek and often in the child's arms. But before long, the animal grew and began to be a nuisance to Goya. He ate the row of corn she planted and the lace cloth she was mending for the church.

"Tie him up," she told the child, but the goat kept on escaping.

Finally, late one night, Goya led the animal across fields, down ditches, and through arroyos to a farm three kilometers away. She woke the farmer, who was a cousin of hers, and said, "Here is a goat," and left before he could offer to pay her back in grain.

For a whole day the child cried, but then he started searching for his animal. He went back and forth in all directions without success. Then one morning he headed for the old highway east of the village. This road, on a steep grade, curved according to the walls of farms and the presence of rock piles and trees.

Patricio paused. "Now we have the new road," he remarked.

"In any case," he went on, "the child walked in the direction of this old road to see if his goat was grazing along it. By coincidence, as he approached, a truck started down from the hills."

Patricio turned to face the widow Bowles. He said that,

although warnings were posted on this road, the truck, without reducing speed, first passed one that said, DANGEROUS CURVE 500 METERS, then one that said, DANGEROUS CURVE 250 METERS, and finally, without slowing down, came to the one where the child sat, that only said, DANGEROUS CURVE, and here the accident occurred.

Now Patricio picked up a lamp and moved in the direction of the *sala*. "The day after the child was buried," he told the widow, "Goya went to the farm where she had left the goat and paid the owner to have it back." Patricio turned from the doorway. "She ties it to her so that it cannot run away."

"I see," said the widow Bowles.

FRAN WAS AWAY from Amapolas much of the summer, while work on her house continued sporadically. Perhaps Sue Ames, realizing Paco wouldn't come until the fall and Fran would not live here permanently until then, lost her previous sense of urgency to finish the job and hand her friend the key. Instead of insisting that skilled workmen leave off cultivating their summer fields to lay floors and make window frames, Sue spent her days in the sun under a wide-brimmed hat, filling canvases with color.

"What is the señora Sue painting?" the widow Bowles asked Altagracia, who was moving slowly with a dust cloth from book to bowl to picture frame in the widow's *sala*.

"Skies," said the girl, whose lean body, Ursula noticed, was losing its depleted look. "All the colors of skies," Altagracia went on. "Red, yellow, purple, orange," though in her experience, except at dawn or sunset, skies had remained largely invisible.

She touched the framed photograph of a man. "Is this your husband?" she asked.

Ursula nodded. "Philip," she said. "Felipe."

"Padre Miguel could pray for the repose of his soul," the girl suggested.

The widow, stunned by a sudden longing to reverse time, touch this Philip's young mouth again, and feel his hand on her young breasts, said nothing.

DURING THAT SUMMER, Fran Bowles spent a week of July, five days of August, and four of September in Sue Ames's extra bedroom. On these visits she saw the widow daily in July, less often in August, and in September, twice.

When Fran first told her mother about Paco, Ursula almost believed she had already met and been charmed by him. He was the third excessively charming man her daughter had loved.

"I look forward to meeting him," the widow had said gallantly. "Do you have a picture?" and she gazed without surprise at Paco's brilliant smile and at the sweater flung over his shoulders, its sleeves knotted carelessly across his chest. Just so had Tom and Andy, her daughter's former husbands, knotted theirs.

Little by little, over morning or evening coffee, Ursula had learned more. Bits of information, like a shower of stones, pelted down on her. Two wives dead, two sets of surviving children and their grandparents, all of them, including Paco, Catholic by birth and inclination. There was the matter of the family name, which shone like a major jewel on the long, tangled necklace of Mexican history.

"Of course, we can never marry," Fran told her mother, "with my two living former husbands."

"Oh no, of course not," the widow said, and she marveled that Frances, so good with maps, directions, and alternate routes, could with Paco have taken so wrong a turn.

As the weeks passed, these conversations became at the same time less objective and less frequent. Fran Bowles, in plain view of the inhabitants of Amapolas, began to avoid her mother.

"Today the daughter brought the mother a tin of imported tea," Altagracia told Sue Ames, "then left immediately."

"They are incompatible," said the people in the village. "Two grown women."

But the widow Bowles, when she looked back later on these weeks, so green with rain, so gold with sun, sometimes caught an echo of her own voice, saying, "Your father and I . . . ," and, "Have you considered . . . ?" Even, "My only concern . . ."

BY THE END of October, the rains were less frequent, though the edges of the roads continued to flower. Seeds clinging to the sharp slope at the end of the mesa had rooted and their flowers starred the weeds with color.

There were still occasional noisy storms, however, usually at night, and on the morning after one of these, Goya, dragging her goat behind her, climbed up the hill to rest in the sun with the widow.

The interval of time passed as always, with silence on one side and talk on the other, interrupted by the serving of bits of food. The widow Bowles sat in a chair that had a view of the lake, while Goya, holding her animal on short leash, took her usual place on the low parapet that marked the edge of the cliff.

"There will be a holiday next month," said the widow, to make conversation, "on the twentieth of November. To celebrate the Revolution of 1910."

Goya nodded, and, as though this affirmation of recollected violence were enough to bring on more, a rocket suddenly exploded in the plaza below. Ursula and Goya rose from their chairs. The goat stood too, alert, his front feet on top of the stone wall. At this moment a female of the species, udder swinging, trotted by on the steep track below. In the space of one second, Goya's rope lost its slack and the widow Bowles, as though she were a soothsayer or seer, divined in detail and in advance all that would subsequently occur. Before the widow could call out a warning, Goya's animal, slit-eyed and obsessed, went over the parapet, with the old woman behind him. Ursula Bowles, leaning from her terrace appalled, watched the bundle of rags that was Goya fall, bound to the goat, down the sheer side of the cliff, head over heels, face up and face down, through clumps of weeds and grasses.

"Did the goat die also?" Ursula asked Patricio later, and learned that the animal had broken a leg.

The widow persisted. "Where is he now?"

"He was shot immediately, to save him pain," said Patricio, whose natural tact prevented him from mentioning the barbecue already planned for that evening in the plaza.

SO FALL CAME on and the harvested cornstalks were tied into sheaves in the fields. At the first frost, the leaves of the cottonwoods along the arroyos turned overnight from everyday green to pale, pure yellow. And by the time of this frost, Fran Bowles's house, which had remained in a state of incompletion throughout the rainy season, had windowpanes, a chimney, and a brick path leading to the door. All that was left was to install, in proper order, first furniture and linen, and then Paco.

Meanwhile, in spite of ritual courtesies, the distance between the widow and her daughter widened and by now was obvious to all.

"But why?" asked Trinidad Gómez, mother of Altagracia and Patricio, adding, "It is not natural."

Why? Sue Ames asked herself. Two intelligent women. It was at this time that Sue, as though it might be a solution of some sort, planned a dinner party.

"To honor the houses on the hill and their occupants," she told Altagracia. "I hope you will help me," and the next time they went together to La Luz, she gave the girl, suddenly no longer a child, money for a dress.

AT THE MOMENT Paco arrived at Amapolas in his red car on the day of the dinner party, the widow Bowles was at the market in La Luz.

"I hate to ask," Sue Ames had said, then explained she had to cook and Fran was waiting for Paco. "Patricio will drive you in my car," Sue told the widow.

Ursula said, "Of course," though she had intended to spend much of the day practicing cordial talk to exchange with Fran's friend. She gazed at Sue Ames, who stood in the midday sun with the market list in one hand while she pushed back the light hair that was blowing around her face. Does she know she's beautiful?

Patricio proved to be a skillful driver, swerving from

animals, slowing for potholes. Ursula glanced at the sculptured bones of his profile and his smooth, narrow hands, and thought, He can't be more than sixteen.

"Do you have a license?" she asked, to which he simply replied that he had learned in the old panel truck of his uncle who raised hogs.

At the market he inserted Sue's car into a narrow space in the shade and, carrying a basket, followed the widow into the vast roofed interior where, regardless of the hour of the day, the light was always twilight.

Patricio had come here often with Sue and had friends in all the stalls.

"Avocados this way," he said, leading her down an aisle to the right. "Pineapple and papaya there," leading her to the left. "Lettuce over here." And with all these merchants, whether friends or not, Patricio bargained, and at length.

Ursula allowed her attention to wander during these conversations. This husband and wife in charge of the lettuce, how was it in their house at night? Were they too tired to laugh and talk? Were they still passionate in their embrace? Was it custom only, and the church, that bound them? Explain love, she wanted to say to the potato sellers, the orange and banana vendors, the blind man hawking peanuts from a cart. All of them must at least have touched its fringe.

Patricio now placed in her hand the coins he had saved by careful buying, and they made their way toward the street. They were almost outside when Ursula noticed a mass of flowers banked in a corner of the enclosure. A ten-year-old girl was apparently in charge of the enterprise, as well as of a smaller sister and a yet smaller brother, who lay half-naked and asleep in a cardboard box nearby.

Patricio will bargain again, the widow realized, and, unwilling to listen, she indicated the flowers she wanted, handed him money, and said, "I will wait in the car." Then she turned back to say, "After you have established the price, I want the girl to keep what is left for herself."

But there was a misunderstanding, and when Patricio came to the car with his basket on one arm and a great sheaf of blooms on the other, Ursula saw that the child had sold him all she had.

THE RAIN, WHICH a month ago had seemingly left off for the season, started again the night of the dinner party and turned dirt roads to mire. I am too tired to go, the widow Bowles told herself as she picked her way along the rough lane, an umbrella in one hand, a bottle of brandy in the other.

But when she walked into Sue's *sala* and three men immediately rose, followed soon after by a fourth, her spirits lifted. Of these men, she had already met Don Enrique, of the *hacienda*, Bud Loomis, co-owner of the land, and the young priest, Padre Miguel. The stranger, of course, was Paco, who crossed the room in seven quick steps to kiss her hand.

Sue had lit lamps and filled her house with branches of bright leaves. As though a stage designer had planned it, the women's dresses reflected these colors, chrome, umber, and, in Ursula's case, pomegranate red. At the revolving center of this kaleidoscope, Patricio, in a new white shirt, was pouring champagne into the glasses of Ursula and Frances Bowles, and of course into Sue's own. All four men, including Padre Miguel, lifted theirs.

A toast to gender, Ursula supposed, offered in unison by these disparate men, each one alien in some important respect to every other. She glanced at Paco, whose arm was linked with her daughter's. The widow Bowles suffered a spasm of the heart. The man's charm, heightened by his stature, his dark red hair, and his broad, guileless smile, was more deadly than she had feared.

Sue, who earlier had placed a dozen candles in pottery holders down the length of her table, now sat at one end behind their multiple flickering. Directly opposite was the widow Bowles, with the heir to the broken *hacienda* at her right. Ursula, with her straight back and smooth white hair, delighted Don Enrique. She reminded him of how he would want to remember his mother, if she had died in her seventies instead of at twenty-six.

Padre Miguel unfolded his napkin at the widow's left. He had expected to be asked to bless the food, but the hostess had said nothing. He decided to thank God anyway and was about to bow his head when Altagracia emerged from the kitchen, a heaped platter of cooked chicken in her hands. And Ursula watched all four men look up, as though they were hunters in a jungle and suddenly some leaves had twitched.

Altagracia, given money and free choice in the city of La Luz, had bought an emerald green satin sheath in which the proportions of her body, its grace and suppleness, and its inevitable effect upon men, were all defined. Skintight, low-cut, preposterous, this dress, with Altagracia in it, aged the child years in a single evening.

Because of the dress, grace was never said. Ursula spoke of Goya to the priest.

"I miss her visits," she told him. "Sometimes I even miss the goat. The substitute child." She paused to look into the padre's face, which remained unmoved and calm. He had forgotten the incident, she supposed, and went on only to say, "I was wrong to let her sit so close to the edge of the bluff."

"None of us can invent the way to change God's will," said Padre Miguel.

At the head of the table, Fran Bowles leaned across Paco to talk to Sue. "Absolutely watertight," Ursula heard her say. "Not a leak anywhere." At that, as though challenged, a flash of lightning whitened the faces of the dinner guests, and thunder rolled and reverberated above them. A downpour followed.

To this accompaniment, Bud Loomis, who had long sat silent opposite Fran, broke in to say he had a red-hot prospect for a sale of land. English people, or Canadian, he said. Or Australian, maybe. Then Don Enrique announced with some ceremony that in January the restoration of the *hacienda* would begin.

"I intend to reconstruct the chapel," he told the dinner guests, upon which Sue and Fran, two agnostics, both said, "Good."

Patricio, unsurprised by his sister's emergence from the chrysalis, continued to circle the table, pouring wine, while Altagracia, lithe and gleaming, hair unbound, lips sealed, changed plates.

All at once Bud Loomis, without waiting for fruit and pastries, looked at his watch, said he had to get going—he had a deal to close—and left.

Ursula, eating grapes, watched her daughter and Sue from the foot of the table. She saw that, of the two, Frances must be ten years older. But wiser? she asked herself. Which of them is wiser? I must explain love to Frances, the widow told herself. Somehow find the words to tell her what love is, what it truly and actually is.

Paco, sitting between the two younger women, was allowing his gaze to rest first on one, then the other. It was now that Ursula Bowles, a reluctant witness, detected a change in his response when he turned to Sue—a quickening, a recognition.

My God, she said to herself. He is abandoning Frances already.

TWO HOURS LATER the widow Bowles stood on her terrace under a full moon. All around her, newly rooted saplings dripped, as did the eaves of her house and the flowerpots she had hung on its walls. A heavy mist rose from the lake, a lighter one from the graveyard.

After the party Padre Miguel had escorted her to her door and paused there with a question.

"Are you not afraid to live alone?" he had asked, meaning, Are you not afraid to die alone?, and she had shaken her head.

The priest carried a flashlight, and when he saw the extravagance of flowers from the market in a pail next to Ursula's door, he commented, "So many."

"Yes," said the widow, without attempting to explain Patricio's mistake. "Tomorrow I'll take them down to Goya's grave," and a moment later she watched the padre's robed, athletic figure disappear on the winding trail that led to the burial ground, the soccer field, and, eventually, his own narrow quarters behind the church.

Ursula, standing on the terrace in her pomegranate red

dress, searched for lights in the village of Amapolas and at last glimpsed one through the swinging doors of the cantina. All the houses were dark and, quite possibly, not only without lamplight but boarded up against the moon, as well.

It was then that she discerned through the mist a number of animals cropping weeds in the graveyard. Cows, she supposed, or goats. She stared into the dark as if the specter of Goya's animal might appear among them.

Oh, love! the widow cried out silently. Who's to say what it is? It's like the verb for *hope* and *wait*. It has no single meaning. She shivered in a sudden gust of wind and, deploying all her inner forces, willed her dead husband back to life here and now, on a stormy November night in the middle of Mexico, at the edge of a garden with a view, and she very nearly succeeded. But even if she had brought him back, she would have forgotten her questions. She would have stood without moving, without breathing, struck dumb, waiting for him to touch her.

Alone and cold in the moonlight, Ursula stepped carefully to the outer edge of her terrace, as though the debris of love, like Don Enrique's broken hand-cut stones, might be lying about her everywhere.

She spoke out loud to the dark. "I might as well measure sky," she said. "I might as well weigh air."

Then, with the moon still high, she began to witness a shift of scene. She saw through the mist a changing landscape beyond the lake of Amapolas, a vast plain where exiled goats ran off to the four compass points. She saw children in tireless pursuit. She saw a whole horizon of dangerous curves.

The widow Bowles shook her head to dispel the fantasy. Below her the shapes of animals, tethered and untethered, moved among the graves.

As soon as Patricio arrived in the morning, Ursula called him to her front door. She had found a round straw basket deep enough to hide the pail, and together they lifted in the flowers once destined for the cemetery.

"Please take them to my daughter," the widow told Patricio, and watched his sure-footed progress with his swaying burden through her garden and out the gate.

Soon after that, Frances stopped Sue Ames and Altagracia as they passed with a casserole and part of a cake bound for the table of the widow Bowles.

"You must come in," she said, and with Paco at her side, led them to the place where the flowers smoldered and kindled and blazed against a bare white wall.

Fran Bowles spoke in Spanish so that all would understand.

"From my mother," she said. "Imagine."

A Over
Middle C

....

AT THE END of April, on the hottest day
of a hot spring, a piano was delivered by flatbed
truck to one of the houses on the hill.

Streamers of dust trailed the truck across the mesa and,
when it stopped, gathered around it in a cloud. This year
of 1964 was already starred in record books. The last scattered rain had dampened the roofs of Amapolas and the
flags of the parade last November 20th, on the anniversary
of the Revolution of 1910. Since then every day had dawned
dry and sunny and darkened into a warm, airless night.

Sue Ames, the widow Bowles, and the widow's daughter
Fran watched from their separate terraces as, noon by
noon, the lake shrank in. Village women, walking tall as

queens under the family wash balanced on their heads, waded across mud shallows to reach shallow pools. Morning and evening, boys with willow switches drove cattle to the center of what was now a pond, where the animals stood knee-deep to drink.

Water from Don Enrique's spring behind the hill was delivered twice a week in metal drums to the houses on the mesa. This source of clean water, known to everyone as the Lucky Woman's Spring, had been named for the owner's female ancestor who was cured of infertility by its waters three hundred years ago.

"These waters of La Dichosa are recognized for their powers," Patricio told Sue one day. "They cure women. In the case of Don Enrique's relative, she died the mother of eight."

Sue cautioned Altagracia.

"We must measure water in half liters," she said. "What is left in the dishpan and the bucket must be poured on plants in the garden."

Altagracia stood in silence, observing begonias and violets wilting in their pots and borders. "Some have already dried up," she said. She lifted a slender bare arm the color of toast in the direction of a few curled leaves clinging to a single thorny stalk.

"That rose, for example," she said.

Sue immediately contradicted her.

"Oh, not that one," she said, knowing she herself would

die of thirst rather than withhold water from the Guadalupe rose.

A column of red ants regrouped at the toe of Sue's sandal. A stunned fly buzzed against her cheek. Lizards slid into the thin line of shade cast by a sapling plum.

Sue moved toward her house. "We will never see rain again," she said.

Altagracia addressed her employer from behind. "Señora, you are wrong," she said. "There will be rain two months from now, on the 24th of June."

Sue turned to watch the girl's red skirt, purple scarf, and ribboned braid drop from sight on the path that zigzagged down the bluff. But almost immediately Altagracia's head reappeared.

"On the day of Saint John the Baptist," she added, and disappeared from view.

Later Sue questioned Patricio when he delivered two letters, one from her mother, one from her former husband.

"How much longer can the village count on getting water from the lake?" she asked, dropping her unopened mail into a small straw basket already crowded with envelopes.

Patricio eyed this basket, originally intended for tortillas. So much correspondence arriving, so little going out, he remarked to himself. Soon these people will stop writing her.

Then he answered Sue's question. "If the lake dries up, the government will dig a well and install a pump," he said, "as they promised in the last election, together with lights for the plaza and modern drains."

Sue looked up at him. These are promises necessary to believe, she realized. And, after the briefest pause, she nodded.

IT WAS DURING this drought, under raw, windy skies, that a new house was built on the hill at Amapolas, directly across the lane from the walled garden of Sue Ames. Bud Loomis had supervised its construction, with the result that it was rectangular, functional, and plain. Instead of including a veranda for the view, or a laurel tree for shade, Bud installed two cement benches on the barren plot of ground.

"Is this house for the Englishman, the Canadian, or the Australian you spoke of?" Sue had asked him, and Bud said, "The Englishman, but he talks more like a kraut."

Sue gazed at her business partner without expression, as though he hadn't spoken. How can you put up with this man? half of her asked the other. How much more of him can you endure? But she had only to look at her house with its carved front door, at her weathered shutters, her stone wall with the green of two olive trees showing above it, and to the distant ring of hills beyond to convince herself, once again, that being here was what she wanted, that the mistake would have been not to come.

Across the short space between them, she examined Bud's square, sunburned face, his obstinate mouth, his startling light blue eyes.

She pointed in the direction of her new neighbor's infertile half acre. "I'll put in some trees," she said, and Bud, astonished by her new decisiveness, forgot to limit the cost and only said, "Go ahead."

So it would come about in a few years' time that trees would shade flowers and vines climb walls at this house where today, April 29th, 1964, a Steinway concert grand was about to be installed, followed two days later by other furniture, and within a week by the owner.

The piano came up the hill on the flatbed truck of Pancho Moreno, the butcher, who brought along his three best friends to help. Together these friends, the Velasco brothers, steadied the roped and blanketed instrument as it made its steep ascent to the mesa.

Word of the piano's arrival spread quickly, and by the time Pancho and the Velascos lowered its gleaming ebony bulk to the ground, half the town of Amapolas was on hand to see if, even without its legs, it would clear the threshold, make the turn, and fit into a corner of the *sala*.

"This is the first piano in Amapolas," said the mayor, forgetting the spinet on which Don Enrique's grandmother must have played rondos and gavottes between candles in the *sala* of the old house.

Polo Velasco, at home in the house of a man he had still

to meet, leaned across the piano he had helped carry in and said, "I could play this instrument. The keyboard of my accordion is identical."

From each of the three houses across the road, a woman emerged. The widow Bowles and her daughter Frances joined Sue Ames at her gate. None of them had expected recitals on the hill. The prospect overwhelmed them.

But when they met the artist himself a few days later, he refused to play, saying, "Please. Not at this time. Thank you."

The piano, however, was not silent. For weeks after the musician's arrival everyone in Amapolas, from the cobbler to the grave digger, from the goatherd to the priest, could listen, whenever they liked, not to scales, arpeggios, and chords, but to the endless repetition of a single note.

Heard on the hill by passersby or through an open window, this note was like a birdcall no one could identify, or the exercise of a mezzo-soprano seeking pitch. Days would pass without its insistent accompaniment. Then, on a sultry afternoon or at night under cover of the dark, it would come, sometimes once, sometimes a dozen times in a single outburst. Drawn from the piano by who knows which one of the old man's fingers, its tone changed from resignation to frustration to hope.

Patricio, bringing letters to the foreigners from the post office, which was scarcely more than a window and a counter between the grocery and the pool hall, remarked separately to each of the three women, "My uncle, who understands such things, believes the musician is suffering from a temporary madness, a *locura*. My uncle says that he himself, in this case, would close the piano and fast for a month." Then Patricio would add, "The padre thinks there is something wrong with the piano and the old man is too obstinate to admit it."

But the padre's visit was unsuccessful because of the language problem. Herr Otto spoke only German, French, Italian, and a few words of English.

"All of us look forward to a concert," Padre Miguel had said incomprehensibly, in the clear, measured Spanish of the seminary. He lifted an arm in the direction of the village of Amapolas and its prospective audience of twelve hundred souls.

When there was no response, the priest went on to ask, "Are you an organist, as well?" and he started to describe the historic instrument in the church, its keyboards, its pedals and pipes, its wheezes and gasps. But, all at once, the elderly musician was on his feet and at his door, bowing and saying, "*A bientôt*." On the basis of the one note that they heard, the people of Amapolas began to refer to the newcomer on the hill as *el músico* or *el pianista*. The American women, once introduced, called him Herr Otto. If they had looked in an encyclopedia of music, perhaps they might have found him there.

"Otto von Schramm," they would have read. "Born in

Vienna, 1889." Seventy-five years old this year, they would have thought, and passed quickly over the names of institutes and academies of music to the names of the orchestras he had played with, and their conductors, to arrive finally at the sites of these performances. The women would have recited out loud the names of European concert halls— Salle Pleyel, Royal Albert Hall, Musikverein.

After meeting Herr Otto, Sue would invent a further past for him, one that included rocks thrown through windows, books onto bonfires, and required travel to unfamiliar places, Auschwitz, Buchenwald, or Belsen.

And though, perhaps, in Herr Otto's case, none of her imaginings were entirely true, on the other hand perhaps none were entirely false.

ONE AFTERNOON DON Enrique, who was fond of light opera, left the supervision of the rebuilding of his house to the foreman and walked across the mesa to call on the musician. He had to knock on the door once, then a second time, in order to be heard above the din caused by the hammering, as Don Enrique would have put it, of one key and that key only. What of the other eighty-seven? he asked himself. Inside Herr Otto's *sala* the visitor sat in a stiff, high-backed chair and spoke of his mother's talent, of the sonatinas and gavottes she played as a girl.

One of his uncles had renounced his career as a violinist to become an executive at the bank. Don Enrique had barely mentioned a great-aunt who sat for a portrait playing the harp when Herr Otto rose to his feet, bowed, and escorted his guest to the door.

"We must expect more heat tomorrow," said Don Enrique.

"*Jawohl*," said Herr Otto.

B Y T H E E N D of May, the earth had begun to crack and the seeded topsoil of the cornfields to be carried off by winds. Tank trucks of water sent to the village by state authorities observed no regular schedule. When cows and goats were milked, flies drowned in the pails. In June the children of Amapolas began to sicken with whooping cough and measles, and infants began to die of dysentery and dehydration.

On June 15th, Ursula Bowles, who was almost eighty and neither desired nor expected much more time on earth, took the direct, dangerous path down the cliff from the mesa to the town.

White hair flying, gray eyes flinty, she entered the office of the mayor, who was sitting, shirt unbuttoned, at a handed-down typewriter, attending to his correspondence.

Her headlong descent of the trail had tired Ursula more

than she anticipated. She stood in the doorway, her back seared by the midday sun, and, to save energy, simply said, "Where is the doctor?"

The *alcalde*, rising from his desk, believed at first that the elderly American was suffering a spasm and brought her a chair, which she waved aside.

She spoke in parts of sentences. "These children," she said. "These years cut off the wrong end of their lives," and paused to prepare further arguments.

"Permit me, señora," said the *alcalde*, wise for his thirty years, pushing Ursula gently onto the chair. He opened a bottle of Pepsi-Cola and offered it to her. He brought her a straw. Finally, he lifted a letter from his desk.

"Today is Tuesday, señora. The government doctor will be here by noon Thursday," he said. "It is a solemn promise."

Soon after that he drove Ursula home in a much-traveled Dodge, circling the base of the hill as far as the road that climbed it and crossing the flat, barren rise to her house on the far side. He had lowered the windows and opened the vents for better circulation of air and, in spite of the interior dust storm that followed, found a moment to ponder the old woman's behavior. A stranger in a foreign land, why should she be concerned? Unless her emotional outburst had been provoked by the fatal illness of a grandchild or great-grandchild in a recent North American epidemic. That's it, the mayor said to himself. That's it.

"How am I to thank you?" Ursula Bowles said when they had reached her house.

"For nothing," said the *alcalde*. Then he added, "The intern will want to meet you," though even as he spoke, he knew this might prove to be a lie.

From the direction of Herr Otto's house they both heard the tolling of a note midway on the keyboard. It tolled twice, once for life and once for death.

LATER THAT AFTERNOON, Don Enrique Ortiz de León was suddenly moved, by the clearing away of rubble and the paving of a large brick area in front of his still-unreconstructed house, to invite a few friends for the following evening to celebrate progress. They could enjoy music, a glass of wine, a laurel tree just planted, and a restored stone fountain, still dry.

Driving his old polished black sedan, he made the rounds of the houses on the hill, stopping first at the one-room, partly finished structure from which Bud Loomis directed the affairs of Lomas de Amapolas Land Development, an informally organized company of which he was president, vice-president, and treasurer, and of which his equal partner, Sue Ames, served as secretary, dealing occasionally with correspondence.

At the entrance to the house Don Enrique stepped over stacks of lumber and spools of wire to arrive at Bud's door, which stood ajar. The lawyer knocked twice and then looked in at Bud's cot spread over with blueprints, his table covered with tools and lengths of tubing, and his two chairs lost under strips of plastic.

The American needs a woman, the visitor told himself, to keep his house in order and to occupy his bed. A woman and perhaps, later on, a child to steady him. But when the owner of the *hacienda* conjured up an image of Bud Loomis striding across the plaza of La Luz with a timid woman and an apprehensive son behind him, he shook his head. No, an arrangement such as his own would more appropriately serve the American's needs. For Don Enrique had long since adopted a pattern of living that suited him well. In his house in La Luz, which was also his law office, he kept old Pepe Gómez as butler, valet, and general factotum and Pepe's daughter Concha as cook and chambermaid. In a separate apartment near a minor plaza of the town, he kept his good friend and occasional secretary, Elena. Leni, as he called her, was a handsome woman ten years younger than himself, of ample body, average mind, and modest expectations. To be weighed against their living arrangement was the fact that it was dull. In its favor was long and easy custom.

This is what the señor Loomis needs, Don Enrique thought, a woman with whom he can be together but apart. On the back of a business card he wrote an invitation to tomorrow night's fiesta and left it in a conspicuous place on a can of paint.

He found the widow Bowles sitting on the parapet of her garden, her glance fixed on the cemetery and its three or four new graves. Sensing despondency, he extended his invitation quickly, in order to distract her. But the widow was not mourning her late husband or her youth or her onetime beauty. Instead, she was happy and, as though it were news of a permanent peace on earth, told him that a doctor was coming to care for the sick of Amapolas.

Don Enrique noticed the degree of her pleasure. She might have been announcing a cure for hunger or a new pill to prevent dying.

"Good," said the lawyer. "I'll invite the *practicante*. The padre can show him the way up from the cemetery." He turned back to the widow from her gate. "Is your daughter in residence?" he asked.

"She will return tomorrow," Ursula said, "perhaps with her friend, Paco," and for no reason, with unexpected suddenness, was catapulted back in time to those early mornings in New Mexico when she had lifted Frances, warm, wet, and content with sleep, from her crib. This is ridiculous, she protested to herself, that was forty years ago. But when she shook hands with Don Enrique, promising to deliver the invitation, the small child's weight still lay heavy in her arms.

Sue Ames was at home, as Don Enrique had hoped. Altagracia admitted him, pointed to the *sala*, said, "There she is," and disappeared. Sue rose to greet him from where she sat on the floor among several boxes of books. The lawyer's internal response was the same one that had troubled him before. Perhaps he was only taking the easy way out with Leni. Perhaps he should break old habits, court this beautiful younger woman, and claim her to grace his bed, under a fine Spanish crucifix, and his board, under his mother's portrait. He saw her in both places and bent to kiss her hand, from which she hastily removed a dustcloth.

"Of course, I will be at the fiesta," she told him, and asked if he would take tea or coffee with her now. But the lawyer said he had a number of invitations to deliver in the village.

"After I call on Señor Otto," he said, and stood for a moment at the front door of this Susahnahahmes, as he continued to pronounce her name. Together they listened to the variations on one note produced by the pianist. "It is the drop of water that wears away the stone," said Don Enrique. "But who or what is this stone?"

He turned back to Sue, who was listening as though to a message.

"There's something familiar about that note," she said. "I've heard it before, played like this, alone."

THE NEXT MORNING Patricio, as though he were announcing a political event, said, "Expect music, speeches, and fireworks." He helped the widow Bowles drag a pot of calla lilies into the shade. "And rain," he added. "This is the day of San Juan."

But the morning passed dry and sere as ever, and the afternoon windless and hot.

"May I bathe for the party in your sink?" Altagracia asked Sue, who said, "Bathe in my tub, but in only five inches of water."

Then Sue returned to her books in the *sala*, but before continuing to dust them, she reached behind her and pulled down a few letters from a shelf. These letters, still unopened, were from her former husband, Tim. Sue took the top envelope in her hand, examined the familiar writing, waited for rage or tears, and when nothing came, dropped this letter back on the others.

Sue found the books themselves to be reminders. Many of them were stamped LIVE OAK BOOKS, the name of the failed enterprise she and Tim had ventured on after his brief employment at insurance and brokerage firms.

But the Live Oak, too, had declined from the start, in spite of a wood fire and chairs in front of it, in spite of tea served all afternoon on Saturdays. Sue had believed this bookstore would prove to be the project that saved them—something they could have in common. But while she offered uncertain customers outstanding first novels and the latest fine work of established writers, Tim, grown increasingly restless, would stalk the aisles between Psychology and Sex, Poetry and Cooking, like a caged beast.

Then he would retire to his office in a cubicle at the rear and angrily file cards marked ON ORDER among those stamped OUT OF PRINT.

Sue, years later, on this June 23rd, sitting hot and dusty on her tiled floor in Mexico, remembered begging Tim to leave his desk. "People want to meet you." And the two would stare into each other's eyes, he wondering, Do I still love her? she, Do I still love him? and separately and silently deciding yes. Or so she had assumed.

THE FIESTA HONORING the resurrection of the *hacienda* pleased everyone present, those who lived beside the lake and those who lived on the hill. The wide paved area in front of the stone foundation was crowded with invited guests, as well as a number of uninvited ones who dropped in to look and stayed on to eat. Old Pepe Gómez, in charge of refreshments, trembling, bent, and for the first time lacking energy to differentiate between them, served the welcome and unwelcome with equal pomp.

"How old is he now?" Sue asked Bud Loomis. "Do you think he's a hundred?"

"Search me," said Bud, and glanced at Sue, surprised as always to notice how large her eyes, how thick her lashes. If she'd only mind her own business, he remarked to himself.

The widow Bowles sat on a bench near the dry fountain with Trinidad Gómez, mother of Patricio, Altagracia, and four younger sons and daughters.

"You have beautiful children," Ursula said. "Especially Altagracia."

Both women turned toward the girl, who was passing food with the grace of a ballerina. Her bare arms were a dancer's arms, her bare legs a dancer's legs. She was wearing her tight green silk dress, which she had shortened.

"May the saints and angels protect her," said her mother.

But she is guiltless, Sue wanted to insist, as though Altagracia had been accused of a crime. She didn't choose to have this mouth, these eyes, these legs.

There now followed, in order, music, speeches, and fireworks. A pair of violinists appeared and throughout the evening strolled about the patio, playing "The Blue Danube," "Song of India," and "A Russian Lullaby." They played "Sobre las Olas" and "Estrellita," and reminded Sue of other café musicians she had heard, diligent and talented masters of their instruments, whose lack of a single quality, genius, kept them from the concert stage.

"Where is Herr Otto?" she asked Don Enrique, and the host surveyed his guests.

"Ah, where is he?" Don Enrique exclaimed. "I extended the invitation yesterday in person." In person and in Spanish, Sue realized. So Herr Otto was still at home, sitting at the keyboard of his Steinway concert grand.

The speeches began, with the host toasting his guests, and the guests, from the padre to the street sweeper, calling on heaven and good fortune to raise the ancient house from its ruins and restore it to its former splendor.

"To the glory of God," proclaimed the priest, lifting his glass and recalling at that moment Don Enrique's promise to rebuild the *hacienda*'s fallen chapel.

While toasts were still being made, the two violinists, taking wine with them, wandered away from the gathering to have a drink and a cigarette outside the wall. Observing them, Sue followed on impulse. She intended to thank them for the old threadbare songs, one or two of which could still trouble her heart. Where was I the last time I heard "The Merry Widow Waltz"? she asked herself. How often did Tim try to whistle "La Vie en Rose"?

She stopped twice on the way, once to be introduced to the new doctor and wonder, Is this the person, barely past boyhood, who is to cure all our ills? She paused again to welcome back Fran, returned from the Mexican state of Veracruz, where she had been traveling with Paco. He was absent tonight and Fran appeared distraught. A few strands of hair flew loose and her gaze was unfocused.

Sue, moving on, arrived outside the wall at the moment the violinists reached for their instruments and began picking at the strings to tune them. At the same time she heard across the wide intervening space of scrub cactus and mesquite Herr Otto's note cast out upon the dark. This note lost nothing as it traveled through the night and arrived remote and clear at the spot where Sue and the musicians waited.

Then as if nothing in the world could be more natural than to stand in a wasteland under stars and pitch their tone to a piano fifty meters away, the two men began to make small adjustments. They tightened strings and tried a phrase or two and, when they were satisfied, strolled back to the gathering, playing "Humoresque."

It was then that Sue, standing next to a high stone wall in central Mexico on a stifling June night, transferred herself to a symphony hall in San Francisco eighteen years earlier.

She sat beside her mother, who looked at her program and said, "We'll have the concerto first."

Sue, ten years old, nodded and watched the orchestra assemble behind a long black piano, saw the first violinist rise to touch one of its keys, and heard sixty instruments respond in unison. The violinist, using one finger, played this note four times, and each time the first violins, the second violins, the violas, the cellos, and basses played the note back to the piano. "He is giving them A over middle C," Sue's mother told her. "Now they are all in tune." Then Artur Rubinstein, trailed by the conductor, walked out from the wings.

Sue, turning back to the celebration, felt a burden lift. The enigmas and frustrations of the last months evaporated.

It is as simple as this, she told herself. Herr Otto has been playing A over middle C. As though he knew violinists would eventually arrive in Amapolas, he has given them a chance to tune.

Sue told Ursula Bowles of her revelation as they walked home under the fireworks.

"Oh, do you think so?" said the widow. But she was distracted by the youth of the doctor she had just met and by the premature appearance of an anxious line between his eyes.

L ONG AFTER IT stopped, no one in Amapolas could agree on the exact time in the early morning of June 24th that rain started to fall in torrents on the town. Patricio said two o'clock, the postmistress said three, and the street sweeper, who slept under the bandstand in the plaza, said the storm awakened him at four.

Sue Ames, asleep until five, heard it all at once through her open windows and on her roof, together with the sound of an eruption from Herr Otto's piano. The moment she heard music, blurred as it was by rain, she reached for a sweater and scarf, and sat at a window in increasing damp-ness for an hour while Herr Otto, through his long French windows, poured rivers of music into the deluge streaming outside.

Sue knew some of these pieces, recognized the sonata

and the scherzo, the nocturne and the fugue, but tonight, in the last of the dark before dawn, found the familiar themes transformed, turned into an accompaniment to the crescendos and decrescendos of the storm. When thunder rolled, she thought she heard a fanfare, when the rain diminished, a chant.

Patricio came at eight under a raincoat woven of *tule* stalks. "*Qué tormenta,*" he remarked to Sue.

"So beautiful," she said. The rain fell steadily for three days, and for a week after that resumed at intervals in drenching showers. Even during the occasional outbreak of the sun, the runoff continued, as did the performances of Herr Otto.

Sue, standing at her gate during temporary clearings, listened day after day while roadside canals flooded with Brahms, and hillside streams with Chopin and Liszt. In her garden, drops fell like grace notes from the leaves of trees.

Everyone in the village of Amapolas sensed himself anointed by the rainstorm. All felt blessed. The priest, who suffered occasional religious doubts, saw in the storm solid proof of God's good will. The doctor was a besieged commander suddenly informed that reinforcements were on the way. The mayor watched the lake fill and tore up his letter to the governor.

On the hill, Bud Loomis covered his leaking roof with a sheet of plastic. During the third day of continuous rain,

Don Enrique was seen on his property, dictating to Elena under a wide black umbrella.

The three American women separately watched the rain fall and separately watched it stop. Separately they listened to Herr Otto's bravura performances.

Altagracia reported to her family. "Each of the three señoras is alone, as if the others had never come. They sit in their houses and think of their men." Then with an instinct mature beyond her years, she said, "The rains have washed their memories. All three señoras, the old one, the middle one, and the young one, can now more clearly recall being courted and kissed."

J U S T   A S   T H E R E was no consensus on the exact moment the downpour started, no two people in the village or on the hill were of the same opinion as to when Herr Otto's music first was heard. Even later on, in other years and other seasons, the matter was never settled. Was it before or after the rain began?

Truckloads
of
Tuberoses

....

SUE AMES HAD noticed Mexican excess as soon as she drove across the border. First, the plethora of junkyards lining the road south. YONKE, read the signs, phonetically. Then a hundred miles of desert. Then a hundred miles of grazing land. Then the sudden green of fields where corn and chiles shared the furrows under steep mountainsides of darkening blue.

The Mexican sky was excessive too, she believed. Wider than others, it stretched over people who appeared no fonder of life than death, as they darted on bicycles between trailer trucks and buses and hurried hand in hand, whole families strong, across divided freeways.

Sue saw connections everywhere, between the eyes of

the tortilla vendor and those of his ancestor the *conquis-tador*, between the profile of the waiter and his close relative the Aztec chief. Mexican animals, too, appeared to have descended by shortcut from their forefathers. Yellow-eyed and ravenous, as if sidewalks were jungle clearings, they prowled the streets of towns, cats with sinuous hostility, dogs with a show of fangs.

So when Sue looked down one summer day at the village below her terrace, she was not surprised to see that the lake had overflowed in last night's rain and that the runoff was creating an arroyo in a neighboring cornfield.

"First too much, then none," she said to her housemaid. "Flood and drought, drought and flood."

"God arranges it," said Altagracia. Then she pointed, "Look, señora, a burial," and she stood with her employer at the garden wall, which had a view of the graveyard below.

"Who has died?" Sue asked.

"The storekeeper," Altagracia said. "Of his lungs," and Sue remembered the lean sober man, whose tobacco-stained fingers had measured flour, sugar, and salt into newspaper twists.

"He died yesterday," Altagracia said. "His son is in the state penitentiary for accidental murder and was not allowed to come to the mass." She observed the gathering below. "You can see the other children. Down there," and she pointed to four hatless boys and three black-shawled small girls, waiting solemnly beside an open trench.

"How will their mother feed them?" Sue asked.

"From the shelves of the store," Altagracia said. "For the present," and Sue saw with her inner eye the grocer's meager stock of bananas, chiles, and tomatoes, saw the empty spaces against the wall between canned milk and cooking oil. "Yes," she said, and contemplated the open grave, the calla lilies that would wilt above it, the young Padre Miguel waiting at its head to recite the worn old words, the widow weeping into her *rebozo*, the seven orphans watching the unfriendly earth receive the man who last week bought them ice-cream sticks.

On all sides of the dead man and the mourners, headstones tilted into weeds. Two cypress trees shaded the crisscrossing tracks of animals, both tame and wild. A crumbling adobe wall bounded the *panteón* and protected the dead.

Sue had started to turn away when she caught sight of a stranger standing in the feathery shade of a huisache tree beyond the oldest graves.

Two months later, when this man and Sue had started to drive together back and forth across Mexico, she would think of him as she saw him first—hatless, motionless, lanky and tall, entirely devoted at this moment to observation. Then she would attach the original image to what she learned at closer range. From her place beside him on the seat of his van, she grew to know his tanned hands, his tanned face, his hair, which was sandy, and his gray eyes, which had a tendency to stare. By then, even blind-folded, she could have recognized him by his infrequent speech and the peculiar resonance that clung to it.

But today, the day of the storekeeper's burial, he was merely a curiosity. What was he doing in Amapolas? Why come here?

AT THIS TIME Sue Ames had left off painting skies. Altagracia had complained of the skies. "How am I to sweep?" And she would wave in the direction of thirty canvases propped against the *sala* walls.

"You are right," Sue said, and the next day piled the skies of all seasons, clouds, and colors in a corner of the storeroom.

"What is this?" she asked Altagracia one day, and held up a canvas smoldering with reds.

Her lovely adolescent employee hesitated. "A sunset," she ventured at last.

"No. It is the bougainvillea on the wall."

Twice that year Sue left Amapolas for months at a time to work with artists in San Miguel. Returned from her latest classes, she devoted herself to sketching faces, first the clear, wide-eyed ones of village children, then the com-posed, secretive ones of their elders.

Once, practicing men's faces, their cheekbones, chins, the sockets of their eyes, Sue inadvertently drew the face of her former husband. She was unaware of this until a few days later, when, sorting through her folder, she turned over a drawing and there was Tim, bringing an unwelcome gasp to her throat.

"How did this happen?" she asked herself. "How could I?" For it was not the Tim of their abrupt and bitter parting, but the original one, the entirely remarkable man into whose arms she had flung herself at the age of nineteen.

The day after this discovery, Fran walked into Sue's workroom and came upon this sketch among scattered others. She took it to a window and examined it in silence.

"Is this someone in Amapolas?" Fran asked. Sue took the sketch from her, pushed it into a folder, and put the folder into a drawer. Then she diverted her friend by asking if the first copies of her newly published book had arrived. And when Fran continued to stare at her, Sue said, "Your travel book," as if the author had written mysteries and poetry, as well. As soon as Fran, still suspicious, said, "Not yet," and left, Sue recovered Tim's portrait and examined it for half an hour.

TEN COPIES OF Frances Bowles's *Your Mexico* arrived a week later and were distributed among the houses on the hill. Herr von Schramm, the pianist whose new house faced Sue's, opened his copy to the title page as though looking for a key signature on a musical score and soon after found a place for it on top of his Bach fugues.

Don Enrique spoke only a few words of English, but ordered a dozen copies of the book for friends who, like himself, could not read it.

As for Sue's business partner, Bud Loomis, he left his copy on the seat of his pickup truck, from which it was stolen. The thief, a ninth-grade student in La Luz, gave it to his English teacher the next day. "A fine addition to our library," the teacher said, and, tall and thoughtless as he was, placed it on a shelf so high only he could reach it.

Patricio Gómez, bringing the mail from the village post office, saw the pile of books in Fran Bowles's house and picked one up. He examined the dizzying jacket. "Three volcanoes so close together and all erupting at once," he commented. "And here in the lava's path, a bull ring." He tapped it. "As well as the shrine of the Virgin of Guadalupe." He tapped that, too. "I suppose this is the cathedral of the Archbishop of Mexico. If he has not already fled, he ought to do so now." Patricio laughed.

"Would you like a copy?" Fran Bowles asked, and signed her name in one of them.

Patricio found a place for *Your Mexico* in the kitchen of his mother's house, between a statue of the Virgin of Light and a jar of manzanilla leaves for tea.

All these people, whether they read English or not, treated Fran's book with respect. Simply to put this many words together was an accomplishment, particularly in the case of a woman. There were only two people who were troubled by it.

The moment it was given to her, Ursula Bowles sat down with her copy and was barely on page two when she said, "No." On page four she said, "No," again. Surely, one does not expect a child on a burro to read a map. Surely, one does not eat fresh cheese tacos bought at noon in summer from a sidewalk vendor. But the next day, Ursula, a mother fearful of rift, congratulated her daughter without reservation.

"A beautiful job," she said. "Really an achievement." Then like Sue Ames, asked, "When do you expect Paco?" changing the subject, but still stepping on treacherous ground, for Paco, the elusive object of Fran's desire, had twice postponed his visit to Amapolas.

But this time Frances had a positive answer. She said, "Soon. Anytime now."

At least for the time being, she has what she wants, Ursula told herself. This book and this man.

Like Ursula, Sue Ames was disturbed by Fran's book. Not because of the author's excesses, but because of its half-truths. Realist though she was, Sue saw Mexico through a painter's eye, converting what was actually there to her private way of seeing.

With the book in her hand, she walked across her terrace to look again at Amapolas. Gazing down at the plaza, she

saw in the afternoon light the pink stone of the Spanish
bell tower and the blue of the dome rising above the laurel
trees. She believed she caught a glimpse through their leaves
of the carved church doors, too, and the street dogs on the
steps in front of them. She imagined a pig or turkey in the
gutter below. And in the square, as if he were actually
there, she saw the alcoholic Gómez uncle, snoring on a
bench. Old Bonifacio, who was blind and begged, sat
nearby on the opposite bench, perhaps for the comfort of
the sound. At the edge of the town, the small lake of
Amapolas gleamed sky blue, adorned like a bride with the
garlands of laundry drying on its shore.

Still holding Fran's book and looking directly at the cemetery, Sue saw visitors at Anastasio Avila's grave. His
widow was there, wiping her eyes on her black shawl, and
the three small daughters, on their knees beside the mound.
At this instant, Altagracia Gómez entered the burial ground
and joined the bereaved family.

Sue, even from this distance, recognized her housemaid's
new *rebozo*. Its colors, which had smoldered in her kitchen
this morning, now exploded in the graveyard. Sue had
never seen so many hostile shades caught between a pair
of tasseled fringes. She had not imagined so fierce a purple
stripe against so venomous a green, so obstinate a magenta
against so furious a pink.

At the sight of this brilliance, the Avila children rose
from their knees to touch the shawl. The grocer's widow

dried her tears. Now Altagracia was exchanging the bereaved woman's black *rebozo* for her own discordant
stripes. At this, the widow stepped back from the grave,
spread her arms to stretch out the colors, and turned twice
in full circles, like a dancer, between the crosses of the
dead.

Sue, unable to see the woman's face, knew that, whatever
she looked like, at this instant she was beautiful.

A moment later, the shawls were exchanged again and
the little group trailed out the gate, the widow in her weeds
once more, the children sober at her heels, and Altagracia
radiant behind.

Not surprisingly, *Your Mexico* sold briskly in the United
States, where people liked the title, the red-and-orange
jacket, and Fran's picture, taken a year earlier, when she
first learned that Paco loved her.

WHEN THE STOREKEEPER had been dead for
a week, Sue carried her sketchpad, charcoal, and crayons
down the perpendicular path to the cemetery. The *panteón*
was empty of mourners. Today, which was the twenty-
first of September, 1965, was one of the majority of days
when no one remembered the dead. Only the Avila mound
was marked by flowers, the calla lilies brought to his burial,
which now drooped limp and discolored above the grocer's
head. But a white cement cross had taken the place of the

temporary wooden one now discarded on the ground nearby. ANASTASIO AVILA, read both crosses, and the cement one went on to enclose his life in a parenthesis of dates. DESCANSE EN PAZ, the inscription ordered him.

Sue sat on an anonymous fragment of stone and had started to sketch, when a shadow darkened the page. She looked up and saw, leaning over her shoulder, almost touching her, the man she had noticed at the interment a week ago. Now, seeing him for only the second time, she was astonished at how familiar he appeared, with his searching eyes, his lean frame, his untroubled attitude. Except for the age difference between them, she might have sat at a desk adjoining his in the third grade. At the beach, as children, they might have dived under the same wave. When she first heard him speak, she thought she recognized his voice.

Now he was reading the inscription on the storekeeper's cross.

"Anastasio Avila, rest in peace," the stranger said out loud.

So that is how it started, in the graveyard of Amapolas, the two of them standing beside a new mound, smelling its rotted flowers, reading the words on its cross. Though both of them, Sue and this stranger, were unaware of it then, this was the first of a number of cemeteries they would visit, the first of a number of autumn days they would spend together.

Sue's encounter with a stranger over the grocer's grave did not go unobserved in the village and on the mesa. Ursula Bowles noticed it from the outer edge of her garden and, unsurprised, was thankful that at last a man had discovered Sue. For, even at a distance and with impaired vision, it was clear to the widow from the stranger's way of standing (*I am willing to wait*) and the quick turn of his head toward Sue (*You are a most beautiful woman*) that this might be the man to rescue her from the ranks of the unloved, among whom she had inserted herself a number of years ago.

Ursula was still contemplating the cemetery when Padre Miguel, followed by some children and a dog, appeared among the graves. The widow watched an exchange of introductions.

"DO YOU VISIT graveyards often?" Sue asked this man (whose name she later found was Charles) when they next met among the headstones.

"Old ones like this, yes," he said. He paused, then pointed to an olive green van parked outside the corroding gate. "Would you like to see the filigree crosses on the graves in Ojos?" And in five minutes they were driving through the plaza of Amapolas, past Padre Miguel on the church steps, the postmistress behind her window, and the intern at the door of the clinic. On the outskirts of the village, Patricio Gómez sped past them on his bicycle and waved.

It was on this first day, when they took a shortcut between towns, that they came across two elephants cropping roadside grass. As at home in an alien land as they might have been in Bengal or Siam, the enormous creatures ignored the car that slowed beside them.

"Elephants," Sue said. She looked up the road ahead, where an old man in a frayed *sarape* was herding a few cows across a ditch. A boy chased a goat into a field. Turning, she saw behind her a single burro, motionless and dreaming, in the middle of the road. All these animals might have been raised in the same corral, so accustomed they seemed to each other.

"They may belong to a circus," Charles said. And it was true that just beyond the cows, some brightly painted vans had pulled off the road into a field. But later on, when she remembered the first time she rode in the green van, Sue would forget the traveling show. In retrospect, for the rest of her life, she would see only the untethered elephants, small-eyed, tough-skinned, exotic, and huge, foraging without prejudice or fuss in a Mexican roadside ditch.

At the end of this first excursion, after an hour spent among the filigree crosses, Charles drove Sue home. No instructions were necessary. "That's my house up there," she had told him, pointing, before they started off, and he had examined the three white adobes on the brink of the mesa, noticed the vines trailing over their parapets and the presence of young olive and fruit trees behind.

"So you mean to stay in Mexico."

"Yes, forever," said Sue. "Won't you?" and he shook his head.

Today, after the trip to Ojos, he left her at her gate.

She turned to thank him, said, "Elephants!" and they both laughed.

He spoke with one foot on the step of his van. "I'll probably be coming this way again next Thursday," he told her.

Thursday came and they drove off together to see the Spanish burial ground behind a church an hour or two away. The following Wednesday they visited the ruins of an Indian tomb some distance to the south.

They had discovered at the start that there was very little they needed to know about each other. He was in Mexico to consult on the building of dams. His full name was Charles MacLain and Sue called him Charles, never Charlie, Chuck, or Chaz, though she believed his school friends probably did. Each knew that the other had been married and no longer was. He supposed she was in her twenties. She imagined he was about thirty-five.

So, week after week, Sue and this Charles traveled in all directions across Mexico, two contented strangers with a picnic basket on the seat between them.

Watching them drive off, Ursula Bowles said to her

daughter, "I wonder if they are in love." At these words, Frances Bowles, still waiting for Paco's visit, behaved as though personally attacked and abruptly left her mother's house, allowing the door to slam behind her.

The priest talked to the intern. "It is unlike the señora Sue," said Padre Miguel.

The doctor made no reply. He was already learning, at the outset of his career, that it was difficult to find any form of human behavior that was entirely unlike any given person.

"An intelligent woman, and talented," the priest said.

The doctor nodded.

"And well-accustomed to living alone," the padre went on.

The doctor said nothing. He failed to nod.

A MONTH LATER than originally planned, Paco sped across the mesa at Amapolas in his red two-passenger Mercedes to visit Frances Bowles and receive a signed copy of her book. Fran had little warning of his arrival, his card having reached her the previous afternoon. Waking at dawn, she spent the morning of the promised day at the market, the bakery, and among the flower stalls of La Luz.

Once home again, she interrupted Altagracia Gómez, who was in the kitchen ironing sheets. "Oh, never mind that. He may be here any minute," Fran told her, and they set to washing vegetables, arranging fruit, remaking the bed. Patricio was sent to the village for matches and candles.

"Why not use your new electric lamps?" Altagracia asked, but Fran shook her head.

Accordingly, Altagracia filled glasses, pitchers, and jars with water and flowers. Then she said, "*Es mucho*. You have bought too many."

Observing the heap of pineapples, melons, papayas, bananas, and grapes spilling over the rim of a copper bowl, she said, "*Es mucho*," again. "Shall I take part of it away?"

"No, don't. Sometimes too much is better," and Fran moved through the house, setting down flowers on tables, chests, the bookcase, and a footstool.

"Tonight we will light the house entirely with candles," she announced in passing.

Like the church during the last power failure, Altagracia thought without saying.

PACO ARRIVED TWO hours late, at eight o'clock, to plunge into the flickering radiance. Sue Ames and Ursula Bowles, parting on the road after an evening walk, detected a new trimness about him, a new purpose in his step.

"Pray for her," the elder agnostic said to the younger.

Inside the house, Paco and Fran, this Francisco and his Francisca, were in each other's arms. But not before he had noticed her spice-brown hair pulled straight back from her fine-boned face and tied behind with a purple bow. Not before she, unaware that he had been sailing for two weeks down Mexico's Pacific coast, noticed his new energy and increased infatuation with life. Embracing her, Paco thought, She still looks young for her age. Frances thought, He has grown younger since we last met.

In the *sala* after dinner, he said, "Let me see this book you have written."

He glanced at the title and the book's brilliant jacket and opened it by candlelight to a random page. Surveying him in profile from her place beside him on the sofa, Frances reminded herself to ask him about his newest project, which involved the stripping away of two square miles of jungle from the coast of a Caribbean cove.

Paco worked as a resort analyst for the Department of Tourism and spent much of his time on planes, searching from above for possible sites of new resorts. After he reported on a promising location, months, even years, of investigation followed. Studies were made of the average temperature, the availability of water, the width of the beach, the presence of sharks, and the character of the natives.

The hotels in which this research culminated shone like pearls strung along the Gulf and Pacific coasts. The tiled floors of their interiors gleamed spotless. Their white gauze curtains, when lifted by breezes, touched immaculate white walls.

In these places, if a guest discovered a cockroach on the ceiling, the chambermaid was disciplined. If a diner bit into a fly in his chicken sandwich, never mind talk of chopped olives, the cook would be discharged.

Now Paco read a page of *Your Mexico*, then read it again. He turned the page and, a moment later, pushed back the candle on the table at his side and reached up to light a lamp that had two bulbs. He turned a few more pages in this new clarity, with Fran close beside him.

At last he spoke. "But, *querida*," he said. "This is not true," and he quoted: " 'To be in this village on its saint's day is to witness an affirmation of faith.'

"*Bellisima*, I, too have been present at this annual fiesta. I remember an accident on the Ferris wheel and a shooting in the cantina. In three hours, four people died. A trained monkey escaped its master and was discovered inside the church at midnight mass, clinging to the Virgin's satin skirt." Paco continued to remember. "Unburied trash blew through the square. A child was bitten by a scavenger dog."

"I was there at another time," Frances said.

Paco pulled the lamp closer to him and turned a page. "But Francisca, *mi amor*, these lodgings you recommend in La Fortuna. We were there together. Don't you remember the damp sheets and towels, the scorpion on the wall?"

Frances said, "Oh, yes," and appeared untroubled.

"When writing of Mexico, the truth is exciting enough," Paco said, and asked himself, How could this woman, who knows so well how to please a man in the bedroom and the kitchen, fold his clothes, and rub his neck, allow herself to be deceived? He looked down at Fran's face on his shoulder and noticed a faint line across her brow, another between her eyes. And at this moment, he realized she was growing old and soft-headed, all at the same time.

The next morning they woke early, lingered in the bedroom for an hour, then breakfasted on three fruits, an assortment of sweet rolls, and a truly excellent coffee.

Paco allowed his cup to be refilled twice, then set it down. "Now I must go," he said. "I am expected in Mazatlán this evening."

Fran protested, then pleaded, but within twenty minutes he was waving to her from his car, as well as to Patricio and Altagracia Gómez, Sue Ames, and Ursula Bowles, who happened to converge in the lane at this moment. Together with Fran Bowles, pale and shaken in her doorway, they watched the red car with Paco in it streak across the mesa and disappear from sight and sound, gone, as the passage of time would prove, for good.

ONCE EVERY WEEK or two, for nine weeks, Sue and Charles traversed the highways and country roads of five Mexican states, stopping not only for graveyards but for his inspection of dams and reservoirs, village chapels and village squares, for their market stalls and the cleared-dirt baseball field at the edge of town. From each of these excursions Sue came home with a sketch, Charles with samples of loam and eroded soil.

They saw no more elephants along the roadside, but smaller animals abounded, as their strewn corpses attested. Calves and colts sprawled there, and every variety of mongrel dog. Once, after dark on the international highway, they saw a dead man on the pavement, lit by headlights. On this occasion Patricio Gómez, who had asked for a ride, was with them.

"Stop!" Sue said, but Charles had already pulled the van out of traffic and was opening his door.

Patricio leaned forward from the back seat. "It is best to continue on," he said. "You can see for yourselves the man is dead."

Sue and Charles, looking back, could not dispute this. The man, who was wearing the white cotton work clothes of a farmer and had a gray beard, lay on his back in the middle of the two-lane road with those cars, buses, motorcycles, and trucks traveling north racing past him on the right and those traveling south rushing past him on the left. His broken *sombrero* lay beside his outstretched arm. He had lost one sandal. His wide stare examined the night sky.

"We will notify the police at the next town," Charles said, and pulled onto the pavement again.

"Yes, let's do that." Sue was watching the two lanes of traffic. No other driver had stopped.

Patricio spoke again. "It is best not to become involved with the authorities. If you report the accident to the police, you may be held as witnesses."

"Held where?" Charles asked.

"In the jail." Patricio extended a hand to rest between them. "For a period of a few days, or perhaps weeks."

Charles drove on.

THAT FALL, SUE and this man explored the countryside of Mexico in all its splendor and distress. They felt the change of season on their skin as they drove through shorter days and cooler evenings. By the end of September, the edges of whatever road they took were lined with tall pink grass, which, as the sun sank, bordered their passage in light.

Often they returned from their excursions after dark, and Altagracia, as she left, would have to light the lamp outside Sue's door. Unfounded rumors began to circulate in the village and on the hill. Then, in November, as they ate sandwiches next to a field of haystacks and sunflowers, Charles said, "I've been called back to Vancouver," and Sue asked, "For good?"

He said, "No, for a conference," and added that these conferences often led to transfers.

"Transfers where?" Sue asked, and Charles, examining a handful of sandy soil, said, "India, Africa, South America, who knows?" When Sue remained silent, he went on, "In any case, I'll be back in Mexico next month for another week or two."

Sue nodded.

ON A PARTICULARLY silent evening half a week later, Sue sat alone in her adobe *sala* and pulled her basket of unopened mail from the shelf. But no sooner were her former husband's letters in her hand than the internal dagger thrusts began. Under a Mexican moon, against all logic and common sense and her own stubborn determination, she allowed herself to remember Tim.

To her annoyance, five almost entirely happy years with him materialized in retrospect, bringing glimpses of them lying on adjacent towels at dusk on deserted beaches, sitting close on seats of cars, standing inside their front door after a party, he entirely wrapped around by her floating chiffon skirt. Sue, staring backward across three thousand miles and these five years, made an effort to remember unhappier times. She thought of Tim's failed ventures as property developer, environmental activist, and proprietor of Live Oak Books. Each enterprise attacked his energy at its roots with broadsides of frustration. He was investigating a shipping business when his father's oldest brother died childless, naming Tim his heir.

"What will you do now?" Sue had asked, and Tim said, "Climb mountains." When Sue made no comment, he amended his statement. "Climb mountains," he said. "For now."

No one was surprised when he learned how and, within six months, was scaling intermediate rock faces.

"Two lucky people," their friends said to each other. "They do as they please. She paints. He climbs." Sue would have been the first to agree.

Thinking tonight of Tim as he was then, smiling, his skin weathered and sometimes scraped, she arranged his letters by date of postmark and opened the earliest one he had written. It was eighteen months old.

"Susie," he began, characteristically direct. "Do you need more money? Please advise. Tim." This must be some new phase, Sue told herself. *Please advise.* Perhaps, after all, he is studying law.

And now, the unfortunate Sunday afternoon—buried, she had supposed, forever—rose up in its shrouds to confront her.

First there was the unforeseen storm, which, after they had parted for the weekend, brought Tim home early from the mountains and Sue back only an hour later from a field trip with her sketching class. Then came her entrance into the house through the downpour by way of the kitchen door. Now, on the hill above Amapolas, Sue saw herself then, putting on a kettle for tea. She saw herself shrug off her soaked jacket in the hall. She watched herself listening to the sound of the upstairs shower. Then the scenes came fast, one after another. Her calling, "Tim?" as she climbed the stairs, her opening the bedroom door, her sight of the bed and the girl in it, a girl with a peeling nose and freckles, who had dropped her boots, windbreaker, and sweater on the floor. Now another sound, of Tim in the shower, whistling as he often did, "Always."

Sue, in her house in the middle of Mexico, understood that all this was funny. Any intelligent person would laugh. But she could not, even now, years later.

Perhaps if Tim had been willing to examine the facts and discuss them, the incident might not have ended in divorce. But he produced a single explanation and kept repeating it. "We were so cold," was all he said.

Sue read his letter again. Please advise, she said to herself, and believed for a moment that Tim was actually seeking counsel. She was reminded of similar beseechings she herself occasionally sent off, not to God, but to a hilltop, a rain pool, a bare branch.

IN EARLY DECEMBER Charles reappeared one afternoon at her door. The temperature had dropped the night before, and, as they took a road bordering a dry arroyo, Sue said, "Look at those cottonwoods!" The brilliance of the leaves, frozen into purest yellow overnight, reduced the rest of the landscape and silenced both passenger and driver.

A few minutes later, Charles said, "This is our last day. They want me in Vancouver tomorrow." He concentrated on the pavement ahead, avoiding slaughter. Then he went on, "For good."

When Sue said nothing, Charles took her left hand in his right and drove on one-handed. In this manner they wound their way for an hour or two past prosperous and derelict farms, past fertile and barren fields, past hay stacked in cones and corn shocks spaced in rows. Sue, mesmerized by this hand, sat mute.

Now, unsought, bits of an old poem drifted into her mind. Something about the instant. The instant made eternity? How did it go? "What if we still ride on, we two? Ride, ride together, forever ride." That was it, or almost.

"It's getting dark," Charles said. "We should start back." And it was as they slowed to turn that she saw the dump truck.

"Look," she said as it swerved past them. "Look at those flowers!"

For here, between the scraped and battered sides of a vehicle designed to carry sand, gravel, or mineral concentrate, lay tier after tier of tuberoses. Tied in sheaves, two dozen deep, the flowering spikes, gathered in a single load like a tremendous offering to an insatiable god, spilled their fragrance into the air and onto the hoods and through the windows of passing cars. The heavy scent of the creamy flowers still hung about the van when Charles left the highway for a shortcut to Amapolas. "We rebuilt a dam near here," he said. But then dark fell and still no signs marked the unpaved lanes. Eventually he stopped the car, got out, and, as though he were Mexican himself, looked up at the stars to find his way.

Finally, he said, "We'll turn here and head south."

They proceeded in this direction for an hour, occasionally asking a man with a cigarette between his thumb and finger or a woman sitting on her doorstep where Amapolas was. But these people still lived in the villages where they were born and had little interest in another settlement God knows how far away.

At last the two tourists arrived at an intersection with a sign that pointed to Los Mirasoles.

Charles stopped in front of it.

"Let's go there to eat," Sue said. "It's in Fran's book."

THE HOTEL, WHICH was called Los Mirasoles like the town, was not lit up, and neither was it cheered by masses of the sunflowers for which it was named. The long, cold lobby, constructed entirely of stone slabs, was softened only by a dozen brown cushions on its benches and six brown-shaded lamps that cast faint circles of light on the black tiled floor.

Charles rang the bell on the reception desk, waited, and when the clerk appeared, asked, "Is the hotel open?"

"Of course." The clerk was a heavy man, bald and sleepy.

"Is the dining room open?"

"Of course." Then the clerk added, "Until midnight."

In this baronial hall, meals were served. A waiter brought them beans and rice that were neither hot nor cold and, after that, a custard that had curdled.

"How did your friend like the food?" Charles asked.

"Perhaps Fran only ate the rolls and drank the wine." Sue looked into his face, and looked away. "Like us."

Soon after that they crossed the echoing lobby and walked outside into the frosty, windless dark. Now Charles said, "Look. Look at that," and wheeled in a circle, one hand above his head. "What a sky!" He pulled Sue to a bench to sit beside him. Then, lost in Mexico in the middle of a moonless night, with a plane to catch the following noon at an airport three hundred miles away, Charles began to explain the firmament.

He identified everything he could see, prominent stars, constellations, the Milky Way, then spoke of the Solar System and galaxies. And all this time, while he pointed with one hand, the other, as it had in the car, held one of hers.

Sue felt she should ask him something. "How many stars are in this part of the sky that we see from here?"

"Directly above us?" He considered. "I'd say half a million, named and unnamed."

After that, he went on to light-years, but Sue had stopped listening. She sat beside him and stared at the side of his face.

"I believe a planet is visible." Charles raised his free hand to point. "Do you see it?"

"I think so," Sue said, and shivered, causing him to bring her sheep's-wool poncho from the van.

She had bought this garment a month ago while driving aimlessly about with Charles. They were in the small town of El Rincón and it was market day. A bent old woman, almost toothless, sold Sue the poncho. "Sheep's wool," the woman said, as if cashmere and alpaca were being offered at the next stall. Sue had touched the stripes, black, brown, gray, and white.

"That's all the colors sheep come in," said Charles. "Buy it."

And now again, weeks later, under a celestial display of extravagant proportions, Charles, having brought the poncho, became practical. He said, "We must leave at once."

But, as things turned out, they did not leave. The desk

clerk had no maps. "You will only drive in circles through falling temperatures," he said.

Sue took Charles aside. "He is only trying to make us take his rooms," she said.

But the clerk prevailed. It was after eleven when he led them upstairs, showed Sue to a room, Number Three, at one end of a corridor and Charles to a room, Number Twenty-five, at the other. He handed them each a key.

"We must have coffee no later than six in the morning," Charles told him, and from his end of the hall he waved to Sue, as from hers she waved back to him.

She hung her clothes on a hand-carved high-backed chair, then waited for sleep in the center of a vast hand-carved bed. At midnight she was still awake, and still awake at one. She lay on her left side, then her right, then stared straight up into the dark. Eventually, she reached to the chair for her sheep's-wool poncho. She pulled it over her head and then walked barefoot down the endless hall to Number Twenty-five.

She was not surprised to discover the door unlocked or to find Charles on his feet, facing it, his back to the window, beyond whose panes stretched the crowded universe, unobserved.

Another
Short Day
in La Luz

....

URSULA BOWLES, WITH more than half the distance to La Luz left to travel, recognized a quick stab of pain below her diaphragm and turned to contemplate the landscape rolling away behind her on the right. At the same moment, Patricio Gómez, her seventeen-year-old driver, as if to confirm that a state of peril existed, said, "There is a deviation ahead."

Ursula turned to see a barrier, lettered DESVIACIÓN, directly in front of them. A flagman waved them to the right, where a rough path, barely wide enough to accommodate a farmer's cart, had been chopped through cactus and nettles. Its dust-filled ruts curved out of sight.

"How long is this detour?" Ursula asked, and found that

121

it continued as far as the town of El Refugio. The flagman and Patricio, standing at the road's edge for a better view, waved in the direction of the southern half of Mexico. Now a pickup truck and the local bus passed them, entered the detour, and disappeared in two separate hurricanes of dust.

Patricio, understanding her hesitation, which would never have been his, leaned into the car and said, "Señora, I know a shortcut."

When another bus passed them, Ursula said, "Yes, let us go that way." She imagined a smooth country lane winding beside meadows and an occasional peach orchard.

They drove diagonally across an uncultivated field, and Patricio remarked, "Besides, we must consider the car." He looked at Ursula gravely. "A borrowed American Ford station wagon, only five years old, with its original paint and tires. Damage might have occurred on the *desviación* from stones like knives and thorns like spikes."

"Perhaps I should not have sold my car," Ursula said, clinging to the door as they descended into an arroyo. "In any case I would not have to borrow. Perhaps I should have driven to Mexico in my own car on some of those roads I used to know." Then, in less time than it took five goats to cross the dirt track in front of her, she installed herself at the wheel of cars in other places. First she drove skillfully around the blind curves and into the gullies of the Mexican mining town where she was born and raised. After that, without a second's pause, she was splitting the flat red earth of a road in New Mexico, speeding down a mile-long, perfectly straight line, with her husband sitting, perfectly, beside her.

Now the last goat crossed, and the widow Bowles was in Mexico again, here by choice in back country on an unmapped road.

"Where are we?" she asked her driver.

"Do not preoccupy yourself, señora," Patricio said. "I know this region well." He turned to stare at Ursula and allowed his glance to rest on her profile. So white-haired, so frail, so slow to decide—was it possible she had steered, accelerated, and applied her brakes on the hazardous thoroughfares of Mexico, fording its barrancas, toiling up its mountain grades? Patricio asked Ursula the question she had more than once asked him. "Do you have a driver's license?"

She found the card in her purse and held it out to him, and even as he drove he examined her picture, her name, and her age. He nodded. "So you are permitted to drive." In this same tone, he had commented to his sister Altagracia, when women's suffrage was made law, "So now you can run for governor."

Ursula glanced at the card. "For two more years," she said, and added, "Someday I'll borrow a car and drive up and down the old roads." And she might have remembered a few of them now, but a sign on the outskirts of a cluster of houses distracted her. "La Soledad," she told Patricio, as if he had no eyes. And ten minutes later she announced, "Los Dolores."

They were traveling along two ruts now, with their right wheels higher than their left, and from her vantage point Ursula discovered herself at eye level with cattle and horses, which looked up from cropping weeds to watch her pass. She put on her distance glasses and made out a church dome and a silo directly ahead and, when they had almost reached the sign, informed Patricio that this was Las Lágrimas. "These names," she said. "All titles of the Virgin, I suppose."

Patricio said nothing. He had never heard of a Virgin of Tears and doubted that there was one. In any case, he saw no point in discussing religion with a woman nobody had ever seen at mass.

Ursula believed that the three names had appeared in natural sequence, and repeated them to herself. Solitude, Sorrow, and Tears.

It was in the town of Tears that Patricio turned left at the cobbled plaza and, as if drawn by a magnet, bounced over potholes and gullies until they arrived at El Refugio and the paved road to La Luz.

Patricio looked back. "The *desviación* is well behind us," he said.

Miles and miles, Ursula silently agreed. But she had enjoyed the detour through the fields and had liked lowering her window to touch corn silk, to smell turned earth.

Even before the church and radio towers of La Luz came into view, Patricio asked the widow, "What must be done in the city today?"

Ursula found her list. On it were a number of items—telegraph office, oculist, and pharmacy—that she did not mention to Patricio at this time. She merely said, "The bank, the nursery for plants, and, of course, the market. I will have lunch at the *posada* while you have a free hour." She believed there was no need for detail. Days in La Luz were all alike, passed in the dim interiors of shops and offices or under noon sun on the crowded, broken sidewalks, in heavy air that smelled of food and flowers.

At the bank, Patricio, who was tall and narrow, stood next to Ursula at a counter marked CAMBIOS and waved her check over the heads of people who had already waited in shifting disorder for more than half an hour.

"We should be given numbers and form a line," Ursula said, but Patricio, extending a long arm and hissing, "Psst, psst," at the cashier, was soon able to hand Ursula her pesos out of turn.

"*Dispénseme*," Ursula said to the pushing crowd as Patricio knifed his way through. "I am sorry. Thank you."

A number of people turned their heads to stare. She is old, she is confused, they thought. What does she mean? Why be sorry?

"I MUST SEND a telegram," Ursula told Patricio, as if the idea had just occurred to her, and a moment later he found a place to park near the office, in the shade.

At Telégrafos Nacionales the dispatcher handed Ursula a form. "You are sending an international message," he said, but his client shook her head.

"The Federal District," she said, and produced from her purse a folded sheet of paper covered with her daughter's dark, emotional script. Frances, hoping to ensure privacy, had written her message in English. Without looking at the phrases her daughter had chosen to lure her lover to her bed again, Ursula handed this paper across the counter to the operator, who unfolded it and said, "This message will transmit more accurately in Spanish." He pushed the paper, together with a pencil and a yellow form, back to Ursula. She heard Fran's words of a few hours ago. "Please send it as soon as you can. It must be delivered today. He is about to leave Mexico City."

Ursula hesitated, looking into the uninterested eyes of the dispatcher. "I would prefer not to read this," she wanted to say. "It is a message I myself would not send." But she knew such an argument would be useless. Why do mothers do these things for their children, especially their grown children? she asked herself, and took up the pencil and started to print.

"Francisco Alvarado Torres," she wrote, putting down Paco's full name, and under that the address of his apartment on the Avenida Victor Hugo in the capital. Even before she reached her daughter's headlong declarations of love and of her willingness to hide and lie indefinitely, Ursula crowded Paco's rooms with various women she imagined. Husky-voiced, wide-mouthed, honey-skinned, they left echoes of perfume in the hall, of whispers behind bedroom doors. And now, in the telegraph office, with a solitary fly circling her head, Ursula placed in Paco's bed her daughter Fran's latest rival—still in her teens, no doubt, product of a convent school, long-lashed, innocent, a virgin until last night.

Frances Bowles, according to her mother's reluctant translation, went on to propose a rendezvous. Wherever you say, she begged. "Please," Fran had written, and "*querido*," in Spanish, as her mother was writing it now.

Pride has abdicated, Ursula perceived, and this raging passion has spilled over into its place. She stopped writing for a moment to ask herself, How was I with Phil? Immediately, an image of her husband, dead seven years, took shape at her side—his profile, complete with broken nose, the top of his head, tan where his hair had thinned. She found herself turning to meet his unshakable blue glance, to reach for his quiet hands, to remember their touch.

What would I do to get him back? she silently inquired of the dispatcher and, as clearly as she could, went on printing her daughter's words in Spanish. "Please," she translated for the second time.

Patricio entered the office from behind her just too late to read the message over her shoulder.

"Now where, señora?" he said. "I am illegally parked."

"To the oculist," she said.

Outside the doctor's door a moment later, Ursula had further instructions. "While I'm here, please select a bougainvillea at the nursery. For the señora who has lent us the car."

Halfway back to the car, Patricio, without taking time to turn, lifted an arm in acknowledgment.

THE DOCTOR'S OFFICE, which occupied the two front rooms of his house, was cool and high-ceilinged. The waiting room had chairs for twelve patients, but all were empty when Ursula entered. Behind a desk at one side sat an utterly beautiful young woman wearing thick horn-rimmed glasses on her sculptured nose and great golden loops swinging from her ears. On the floor at her side, a boy of three or four, identical in profile and wearing heavy glasses of his own, played with the boxcars of a wooden train. The woman and child looked up as Ursula entered, and examined her with the myopic, spice-brown eyes.

"I have an appointment with the doctor," Ursula told the receptionist, whose name, according to a lettered sign on her desk, was Griselda. But before there was time for a response the telephone rang and a conversation followed.

Griselda looked up. "Forgive me," she said. "Your appointment is canceled. There has been a death in the doctor's family," and at this, as though a floodgate had burst open, the calls began to come incessantly. Occasionally, Griselda had time for a few words of explanation. "The doctor's mother," she would say, or, "Eighty-six years old," or, "After high mass, the interment. Gallegos Brothers in charge."

Listening to the receptionist, Ursula reminded herself to talk to her daughter again. Though how could Frances have forgotten? On matters such as this, mother and child were in accord. No services or ceremonies—simple cremation, with the small sealed box that resulted carried across the border to the southwestern hillside where, three years ago, living in New Mexico, she had taken Phil's. Nothing could have seemed more plain and ordinary at the time she had planned it, but today in La Luz, with church bells tolling the hour of one, a priest and four nuns visible through the doctor's window, and Griselda's repeated references to a cortège and the *panteón*, apprehension began to gnaw at Ursula. Would there be obstacles in a Catholic country? I must tell Frances again exactly what I want, she told herself, even if she is frantic about Paco. I must write it down and sign it.

While Griselda gravely informed callers of funeral

details, Ursula, followed by the child, left her chair to study a group of framed pictures on the wall opposite the desk. She was surprised to find they were all of the same subject—a happy woman's round, cheerful face. But each portrait in the series of identical poses was flawed. One was almost entirely obscured by mist, one streaked by random clouds. An opaque black center half filled another. A wide circle of black hid most of the fourth.

"What do these pictures mean?" Ursula asked Griselda, who at last had found a moment to open her appointment book.

"They show how people see who have diseases of the eye," and Griselda went on to name some of them. "Astigmatism, cataracts, detached retina." She seemed to chant. "Glaucoma, macular degeneration."

Ursula lingered before the pictures, hypnotized. Silently, the child was separating the boxcars, one by one, from his train when Patricio burst in, leaving the door open to street dust and sunlight. "¿*Qué tal?*" he said to the bespectacled child, and "*Vámonos*" to Ursula, who, taking an appointment card from Griselda, hurried after him into the midday crowd.

"Are you losing your sight?" Patricio asked as soon as he and his passenger were in the car.

"Oh, I think not," Ursula said, and then, "What is that smell?" Twisting in her seat, she saw that the entire space at the rear of the station wagon was wound about with a tangle of flowers and vines.

"Besides the bougainvillea, there are three honeysuckles," Patricio said, and he, too, looked back. "They are gifts from the proprietor of the nursery, because you and the other North American señoras buy so much from him."

The combined fragrances of the nurseryman's gifts were almost suffocating. Ursula lowered her window. "Where to now?" asked Patricio, and after a small pause she said, "The pharmacy."

Patricio offered his help. "I can make this purchase for you while you rest in the patio of the hotel." Ursula shook her head. "I prefer to do it myself," she said.

From the driver's seat, Patricio observed the passenger beside him. So rich and old and weak, he remarked to himself, and so obstinate.

Before entering the pharmacy Ursula handed him a shopping list and a quantity of money. "This should cover everything," she told him. "What you buy at the market, and your own lunch, as well." Then, as though noticing his habitual leanness for the first time, she asked where he ate in La Luz.

Patricio said, "At Un Taco Más," though in actuality he intended to take his midday meal at the house of his mother's cousin and save this money for an emergency.

"Let us meet at the *posada* at three," Ursula said, and watched him turn the corner in the flower-scented car.

THE FARMACIA BUEN Salud was situated next to a music store. Even inside the pharmacy, strains of music could sometimes be heard when a patron of one shop and a patron of the other opened the street doors simultaneously.

Ursula, stepping from the shadeless glare of the sidewalk into the shadowed room, thought at first that she was the pharmacy's only customer. Then she saw the proprietor at the far end of the counter, attending to a bent old woman who was wearing two shawls, two skirts, and no shoes. In his hand was a glass of water and a bottle. His ancient client held up a bony forefinger, and the pharmacist shook out a single pill. Ursula watched the old woman extract coins from a knot in her *rebozo*, lay them on the counter, pick up the pill and the glass, and swallow.

The pharmacist, a man with a brooding air of disillusion, now approached Ursula. "Can I help you, señora?"

In order to conceal the true purpose of her presence here, she began with ordinary purchases. "Adhesive tape," she said. "Hand lotion, a toothbrush."

The pharmacist collected these things and placed them on the counter. "What more?" he said.

Ursula, looking first at a display of cough syrup, then at an apothecary jar filled with a purple liquid, eventually said, "Something for pain."

"Do you have a doctor's prescription?" he asked, and she shook her head.

Through his somber eyes, the pharmacist examined her face. "Where is the pain?"

Ursula waved vaguely at the area between her shoulders and her hips. "What I need is something stronger than aspirin," she said.

The pharmacist allowed his gaze to rest on the apothecary jar.

"Consider this, señora," he said. "I cannot diagnose the cause of pain. I can only sell the medicine to alleviate it."

"That is all I ask of you," she said.

The pharmacist then disappeared into his dispensary and came back with white capsules.

"No more than two a day," he instructed her. "And here are the cards of some excellent local doctors."

At this mention of local doctors, an image of the recently installed government intern at Amapolas sprang into Ursula's mind. She saw his young face, his troubled eyes. "Señora, are you losing weight?" the intern had asked.

At the moment when Ursula pushed open the pharmacy door, two customers entered the music shop. From the sidewalk she heard a mariachi band playing "Ojos

Tapatíos." "How I love that song," she said out loud in English, and a passerby turned to stare.

THE POSADA DEL Sol was only five blocks from the pharmacy and Ursula was halfway there when she noticed a sign on her left. GALLEGOS HERMANOS, FUNERALES, she read in gold-and-black letters on the glass front door. Seeing this as a lucky encounter, Ursula crossed the street. She found the three Gallegos brothers standing together just inside the door.

They bowed, shook her hand, and asked her to come back at four. "It is past the hour for lunch," they told her, and pointed to a clock with golden hands and a golden pendulum as witness.

"I have only one simple question," Ursula said, and held up her right hand as though to detain them. She merely wished to know if their services included cremation, but the necessary words were not in her vocabulary, and in the end she simply said "fire" and "burn" and, a moment later, "ashes."

The Gallegos brothers, black-suited and bald, were shocked into silence by this stripping away of euphemism. This old woman, so close to death and to purgatory, said the eyes of each to the eyes of the others. So willing to disappear into eternity and leave no trace behind, their eyes agreed.

"You are disturbed, señora," said one Gallegos.

"Let us talk later," said another.

"Yes, after lunch—at four o'clock," said the third.

They bowed, escorted her to the door, and called out after her, "Until then."

SEATED IN THE dining room of the *posada* at a small table in the rear, Ursula reached into her deep straw bag for the pharmacist's pills. This was the time to take one, for she was alone, had just now suffered sudden pain, and had a glass of water at hand. But all at once a man was at her side, saying, "Señora, will you join me?" and here was Don Enrique Ortiz de León. Ursula, wearing her reading glasses for the menu, stared up at him half-blindly, then removed them and noticed how handsome the heir to the *hacienda* at Amapolas still was. Straight brows, straight neck—he reminded her of something, perhaps an eagle.

If only Frances were attracted to a stable man like this one, she found herself thinking, and then, imagining the two together, Have I gone mad?

Three minutes later she was at his table. Don Enrique, without wasting time, ordered seviche, tortilla soup, and rice with chicken for them both. "And *vino blanco*," he told Violeta, the new waitress, long and slender as a sugarcane stalk.

Ursula protested, "Oh, no, I can't eat so much," but

Don Enrique, choosing not to hear, merely passed her the hard rolls. "*Salud*," they said to each other when the wine came, and they touched glasses.

"Have you accomplished all you wished to do in La Luz?" he asked.

Ursula, thinking of the oculist, the pharmacy, and the Gallegos Brothers, shook her head. Only the cashing of the check, the purchase of the bougainvillea, and the sending of the telegram were done. As for the three other matters, much remained unresolved.

"The oculist had been called away," she told him.

Immediately Don Enrique, like Patricio, said, "Are you losing your sight?" and again she answered, "Oh, I think not."

"My mother was blind for a year before she died," Don Enrique said. "Her hearing became so acute that she could identify visitors by their footsteps alone, long before they spoke."

The widow knew she would try this. One day, she would close her eyes and, using the correct name, say "Good morning" to her daughter and Sue, to Altagracia and Patricio, the priest, the doctor, the mayor.

Don Enrique ate slowly, and slowly drank three glasses of wine. He spoke of the weather and the economy.

Then all at once he turned and waved a hand to the wall behind him. "You have noticed the portraits painted by our neighbor Susahnahahmes."

The widow, understanding that he was speaking of Sue Ames, found her distance glasses, focused, and there was Sue's work, five heads of children, possibly Amapolas children.

"She is too modest," Ursula said. "I didn't know." And she silently berated herself for choosing to be remote, even from the handful of people on the hill at Amapolas.

"Look, señora," Don Enrique said. "You can read these children's eyes," and the widow, even with imperfect vision, saw that this was true. The eyes of these faces held nothing back.

A shadow fell across the table, and Ursula, looking up through the window, observed a gathering of clouds. Certain she could eat no more, she laid down her fork. "You have always lived in this town," she said to her companion.

"No, no," he said. "As a child I traveled abroad with my parents."

"Where did you go?" Ursula asked, and at this, to her astonishment, a torrent of recollection poured from Don Enrique.

"To the Eiffel Tower," he said, "the Tower of London, the Alhambra, Napoleon's tomb." Don Enrique went on, "And the restaurants." He named a few, and Ursula began to recognize, in his voice and in his eyes, the banked embers of nostalgia. At the same moment, as though a contagion had spread in the dining room of the Posada del Sol, the widow fell into her own fever of recall.

"Did you ever eat at the Ferme Saint-Jacques, in the south of France?" she asked him, but he shook his head and went on to remember the Leaning Tower and the Roman Forum. With attentive eyes on her host's face, Ursula Bowles withdrew to a hill above the Mediterranean, where she sat at a table with her husband, Philip, at the outer edge of a flagstone court. On one side of them more diners sat at tables; on the other an abrupt slope, terraced with grapevines and olive trees, dropped straight down to the sea.

Half listening to Don Enrique and wearing a fixed smile, Ursula fished the depths of her memory to discover the exact blue of the sea that day. How was it then? she asked herself. How was that day in France?

Peering through her memory's eye, she believed she saw short-stemmed field flowers crowded into a shallow bowl on the table. She recalled earthenware plates and copper pans. What were the Gallic miracles they ate? What was the ambrosia that they drank?

But clearer than the food, clearer than the wine, what Ursula recovered at this instant, four thousand miles from France, was the accurate image of their waiter on that sapphire day at the Ferme Saint-Jacques. So sharp were the outlines of this hallucination that he might as well have been standing beside her here, in this other dining room.

The French waiter was wiry, lithe, and fierce. His eyes blazed a passionate black. He wore a pirate's sweeping black mustache. Ursula watched him bound up and down the steps to the kitchen. She thought she remembered the courses he brought—the pâté, the soup, the fish, the young lamb, the wines. "All this is from the *ferme*," the waiter told them. "The wine, too," And the young Ursula and the young Philip nodded, trying to believe. Now the sun sank away from its zenith, the day declined, and the Bowleses asked for their bill.

"We can eat no more," they told their waiter.

"There is still dessert," he said, then he sternly recited the choices.

"We cannot. It is impossible. *L'addition, s'il vous plaît.*"

At this, heads of thrifty French at nearby tables turned to stare, for there was a fixed price.

"One moment," the waiter said.

"He has gone for his cutlass," Ursula told Philip.

But he returned quietly with two plates and five platters. "*Les cinq desserts obligatoires,*" he said, and he placed a spoonful of each on the plates.

From a provincial town in Mexico, the widow Bowles, bending her glance around the curve of the earth and finding the south of France, conjured up the waiter's quick black eyes, his wide smile white with teeth.

Don Enrique interrupted. "You are smiling," he said. "You, too, have traveled to Copenhagen," and she nodded, though it was a city she had never visited.

"We will both have *flan*," Don Enrique told Violeta, who for half an hour had hovered patiently nearby.

The widow rose from her chair. "Oh, not for me," she said. "Thank you. You have been so kind. But I believe Patricio is here," and, as if to prove her truthful, her driver entered the hotel at this instant and could be seen standing restless in the lobby.

"You are late, señora," he said as they walked to the car. "The lettuce and spinach are wilting and the strawberries are beginning to rot." He opened the door on the right.

But halfway there Ursula stopped. "I will drive," she said. Patricio handed her the keys.

A N D   S O   T H E Y traveled the road back to Amapolas. As she drove, Ursula was aware of an unexplained delight trembling in her bones. She made no attempt to analyze this sensation, but for an hour or two it turned her young. She sped down the highway to each arroyo and up the grade to the next rise. The tangle of flowering vines, their fragrance subsiding, occupied the rear of the car; three market baskets, heavy with fruit and vegetables, filled the back seat. Looking straight ahead, Patricio sat somberly beside her as she passed trucks and slowed for burros. Ursula understood his mood. For the time being, his only wish was not to be seen as a passenger in a car she was driving.

They left the highway twice, once to buy gas and once for another detour. At the gas station, a boy of six removed his shoes, climbed onto the hood, and polished her windshield with his shirtsleeve and a wet newspaper. Patricio watched her hand the child coins.

"Señora, you tip too much," he said, and, a few moments later, "Another *desviación*."

The detour they had to take, unlike this morning's, was short. They traveled through its dust for only a few miles. When they were at a midpoint, Patricio said, "On the right is my great-uncle's farm." And he went on to give Ursula further family information. "When my great-uncle knew he had cancer and could not wait to die of it, he hanged himself in the *bodega*." Patricio pointed to the storeroom, a square adobe structure behind the longer low adobe house. "In there," he said. "By a rope from a rafter. One of his grandchildren found him. Carlos, seven years old." Patricio's eyes were on the widow.

She said, "What a terrible thing."

Patricio had more. "Now Carlos has lost his speech."

And Ursula said, "Poor child."

"Two weeks have passed since the suicide," Patricio went on, "and still not a word from Carlos."

But the widow Bowles did not rage against fate, as he

had expected. Instead, she accepted this tragedy. She might have been Mexican herself.

Ursula understood that Patricio was punishing her, and, once back on the paved road, she changed places with him. So she was not driving when the pain, now grown familiar, struck again. Later on, she would take the first pill.

BY THE TIME they reached the house on the edge of the mesa at Amapolas, dusk was coming on. Patricio carried in her basket and one pot of honeysuckle and drove away to deliver the rest.

But before leaving he commented on the trip. "Another short day in La Luz," he said. "Only a few hours, and so much done."

As soon as he left, Ursula went to her terrace to watch the day end. She saw that a sunset had begun to streak the western sky with color and turned to look for its reflection, like an echo, on the opposite horizon. Only when she moved a chair to face the eastern hills did she realize how tired she was, and at the same time how oddly filled with joy.

Today had stopped happening. Already it had consigned its events to memory. Untouched by the evening chill, she sat outside until dark, wrapped in the mists of her brief, uncertain future and the brilliant patchwork of her never-ending past.

Bud on the
Side of
the Angels

....

BUD LOOMIS HAD lived for several years on the western edge of the mesa in a simple square house that was scarcely more than an adobe block. Unadorned by shutters, tiled casements, or even a chimney, it was the architectural counterpart of its owner, rough, solid, and defiant. Beyond and below this house, a two-lane paved road ran north, eventually to join the international highway that led the traveler to El Paso, Texas, USA.

Sue Ames, crossing the mesa on a searing April afternoon, could see Bud's house at the opposite end, could see its door and a gleam of water. Altagracia Gómez must be emptying the dishpan. Bud's pickup truck was not to be seen. So I can talk to her alone, Sue observed with relief.

About the three starving children. She stepped ahead more quickly, passing on her right the adobe villa of the elderly American sisters who intended to spend winters on the heights above Amapolas. Due to a misunderstanding and contrary to the usual way of things, their house was completed eight months ahead of time and would stand empty until December. Sue believed that spiders were already festooning the doorways with their webs and field mice tracking the kitchen shelves.

She went on until the solid walls of Don Enrique's house stood on her left, then paused in front of the long, low dwelling of his nephew. This nephew, who speculated in real estate, had bought the property on the basis of his uncle's forecast of its rising worth. But a year later, the nephew was still waiting to double or triple his investment, on which he paid high interest to the bank. Twice a month he brought his reluctant wife and children from La Luz to picnic on the property. Here his family, removed from the cinemas, parks, and sidewalks of the city, was forced to endure the tedium of the country while the father strolled about the mesa, filling a legal pad with projections of profit and loss.

Now Sue approached the third new house, built by an Australian couple and sold before occupancy to a former mayor of La Luz. As soon as he took possession, this retired government official constructed a *frontón* court for jai alai and began excavation for a swimming pool. The crew he brought from La Luz had dug this pool to half its proposed depth before they learned that neither the lake of Amapolas nor the hillside spring could provide the water to fill it.

The excavation, which was visible to the passerby, was never refilled, its rocky contents having already been spread out to level projected lawns and rose beds, and over the past year it had become a repository for rubble, cactus, and seeds dropped by birds. It might appear unlikely that this pit of discards could turn, during a single season's rain, into a sunken garden, but here it was. The excavation barely contained the green tangle destined soon to overflow it. A morning glory in full bloom clung to the thorns of a nopal cactus and the spikes of a maguey. A honeysuckle vine had obscured a mound of broken bricks. Tall weeds were flowering chrome yellow.

Ahead of her, across three properties yet unsold, Bud's house stood square and uncompromising at the edge of its barren plot of land. His maid of all work was not in sight.

Ah, Altagracia, Sue mourned to herself. You were beautiful to have around my house, even on the day you left me.

ON THAT DAY two months ago, Altagracia, in a purple skirt and a scarlet *rebozo*, her lashes fringing her direct black glance, had announced, "This is the last time

I can work for you, señora. Señor Loomis has employed me for five entire days a week." Then, allowing her astonished employer no time to answer, she pulled a child into the kitchen from the doorstep. "This is my sister, María del Rosario. You can call her Chayo."

"But she is so young."

"She is twelve, my age when I came to work for you."

Sue shook the smooth, narrow hand of Chayo, who, in proximity to her sister, was a candle flickering beside a torch.

"So you are sixteen now," Sue said, and asked herself, Wasn't that the age they all were, Juliet and Ophelia, Rapunzel and Rose Red?

Chayo had worked for Sue and the two other North American women no more than a week before a series of thin little girls began to appear with her.

"Who is this?" Sue would ask as the children, one by one, were brought to meet her. And Chayo told her, "It is my cousin, María de los Angeles. She will help me dust. You can call her Chela." Or, "This is María de la Concepción. She can dry the plates. Call her Concha," or, in the case of the third, simply, Lupita, which everyone, even foreigners, knew was short for María de Guadalupe.

Chayo gave their ages. "She is ten. She is seven. She is five. In the morning she will help me. After lunch I will take her home."

Sue sometimes entered the kitchen at noon and, when she saw how fast that day's helper ate, suggested second servings. She watched Lupita, kneeling on a chair at the kitchen table, scoop up beans, rice, and slivers of beef with a tortilla and her fingers.

"Slice her an orange," Sue instructed Chayo. "Give her a piece of papaya."

One day, Sue, realizing Chayo's three cousins were sisters, questioned her. "Do they have enough to eat at home?"

Chayo hesitated, then replied with a single word in the form of a question, "*¿Sabe?*" By eliminating the *quién* from *quién sabe*, the *who* from the *who knows*, she succeeded in implying that the plight of the children was of no importance either to man or to God.

AT BUD'S HOUSE Altagracia led her former employer into a combination *sala*, office, and bedroom, where some order had been achieved by transferring tools, survey maps, and correspondence into boxes now stacked against a wall.

"Altagracia, how have you been?" Sue asked unnecessarily, for Bud's housekeeper shone, from hair to skin to lips to eyes. She's in love already, Sue confirmed to herself with a pang, and about to be badly hurt.

At this moment, Bud Loomis, as though pushed from

the wings by a stage director, strode in, knocking over his desk chair and leaving a trail of boot prints on the newly mopped floor.

"Long time no see," he said to Sue.

She explained she had come to ask Altagracia about her cousins and, turning to the girl, said, "These children, do they have enough to eat at home?"

Altagracia, her brilliance dimmed, looked down to examine the floor, then said her cousins did not eat at home, because her aunt could not buy food. Her husband was away.

"Away where?" Sue asked.

"*En el otro lado*," and Altagracia lifted a hand to point north, in the direction of the barbed-wire border. "He went to pick fruit."

"And he cannot send his family part of what he earns."

"For two months he sent almost all. Now the letters still come, but without checks."

"He has had expenses," Sue said, thinking women, bars, slot machines.

"But he writes of money, señora. 'With what I send you, pay this month's rent,' he says. 'Buy shoes. Pay the store.' But he has forgotten to send the check."

Sue was silent for a moment. Bud, behind her, his face flushing, was silent, too.

"Have the envelopes been opened?" he asked.

"*¿Sabe?*"

"Judas Priest! What's going on?"

The two women watched as this explosive man surrendered himself to rage, loudly calling on God and Jesus. When Altagracia told Sue the cousins numbered five in all, Bud shouted, "Christ!" with such passion that Altagracia believed for a moment he was praying.

Muttering, "Bastards!" Bud stormed out of the house, into his pickup, and down the hill to the village plaza.

The postmistress, Carmen Ruiz, daughter of the former postmistress, old Carmen, sat in her usual place behind the counter, facing the door and the plaza. Carmen knew certain secrets of the people of Amapolas. She could tell you which ones were able to read and write and which were not. She could say which ones communicated with relatives and which ones never bought a stamp. She separated the richer from the poorer by examining the paper they wrote on.

Carmen the elder had resisted retirement until her daughter was promised the job. This transfer was accomplished through the good offices of Don Enrique, who remembered that the great-grandfather of the applicant had been the first to warn his family at the *hacienda* of the approach of Francisco Villa and his men. Horacio, the husband of Carmen the elder, had worked as a clerk in the land-tax office.

"These Ruiz are never without federal government positions," the people of Amapolas remarked to each other.

Carmen the younger was a product of new times. She

dyed her hair brick red and painted her fingernails to match. She longed for rhinestone-buckled satin pumps and a jacket with a fur collar.

On that afternoon when Bud burst into the post office where Carmen sat, newly manicured, behind the counter, she barely had time to say, "Nothing for you today, señor," before he fired off his arsenal. Words barely known to her in Spanish and unknown in English exploded around her and so assailed the ears of Padre Miguel, who entered at this moment, that he quickly backed out into the street.

In spite of its fury, Bud's invective failed to jar Carmen's complacency. Steam open an envelope? Forge a signature? Please remember she was a Ruiz.

The next morning, Bud Loomis, with Altagracia at his side, drove to the grocery store of the widow Avila. Allowing the motor to run, Bud pushed into the dim, narrow shop. Without wasting time, he gave Anastasio Avila's widow his order. "Candy," he said. "All you've got," and three minutes later was back in the truck with Altagracia, a sack of peppermints, lemon drops, and caramels on the seat between them.

At the desolate dwelling of the Gómez relatives, a single sinewy rooster stalked the dooryard, where the five children were inventing games in the dust with stones. Now appeared Altagracia's aunt Ofelia, a woman clearly on the brink of something—starvation, surrender.

Altagracia made short work of introductions. "This is

Señor Loomis," she said. "He believes he can recover your money." And before Ofelia could either weep or thank, Altagracia added, "He must have more information, the name of the bank, the dates."

Half an hour later, while walking to his truck, Bud noticed the children surrounding the sack of candy as if they had been appointed its custodians.

"Eat, for God's sake," he said.

In early May, one day before a national holiday, Bud met Don Enrique for lunch at the Posada del Sol in La Luz. The Mexican gentleman, who had served Bud and Sue Ames as legal counsel from the beginning, was familiar with Mexican business practices and the customs and traditions that regulated them.

Don Enrique was already sitting at a window table and being served Coca-Cola without ice by the willowy Violeta when his client arrived.

"*Ciao,*" Bud said, sitting down.

This man is becoming more of an enigma each time we meet, Don Enrique remarked to himself. In the square outside, a few musicians, rehearsing for tomorrow's band concert, practiced trumpet fanfares.

"I'd like to meet someone at the bank," Bud said, tearing his hard roll in half. "The manager or a vice-president. Someone like that."

"My second cousin is the president," Don Enrique said, and left the table to telephone for an appointment.

Fragments of trumpet calls from the plaza accompanied his passage.

The meeting went well from beginning to end. First, Don Enrique and his second cousin discussed family matters, the whereabouts and state of health of relatives, new births to cousins, and approaching deaths, then touched on civic affairs, the state of the street lamps, the disposal of sewage, the shortage of benches in the square. At last, the banker reluctantly turned to Bud and, fearful of having to approve a large personal loan, asked how he might help him.

When Bud said, "I am tracing stolen money orders," the two relatives stared at him, for the North American bore none of the earmarks of a private investigator, being neither suave nor subtle. All this man could boast was his stubborn jaw and his fixed blue stare.

"Were these stolen money orders made out to you?" the banker asked, and when Bud said, "No. To Ofelia Gómez, wife of Juan Ramos," the cousins' eyes met. So a woman was involved.

"Who is she?" Don Enrique asked, and Bud explained that Ofelia was Altagracia's father's sister.

"Oh, yes," Don Enrique said, searching his memory. He prided himself on knowing everyone in Amapolas, particularly those whose forebears had served as retainers to his family.

"One of old Pepe's descendants," the lawyer told his relative, and went on, "the aunt of Patricio and Altagracia Gómez." No sooner did he speak these words than he understood everything. He, too, had seen Altagracia enter and leave Bud's house on the mesa, had watched her walk away in beauty that, step by step, only seemed to grow. He had also observed Bud in his doorway, gazing after the girl until she was out of sight. So in this case, the mother of five hungry children, as Bud had described the aunt, was scarcely involved. Bud had needed only to know that they were relatives of Altagracia, this person who, even when she walked past without speaking, caused the air to flower and the silence to sing.

Now Don Enrique, in full comprehension of the situation, asked Bud for details.

The North American reported that Ofelia had received eleven letters from across the border. From Stockton, California, to be precise. Of these, only the first two arrived with checks enclosed, though money was mentioned in all of them.

"Nine checks are missing so far," Bud told the two cousins, who observed his deepening flush with some alarm. Would the property developer actually suffer an attack here, in the bank president's office?

Don Enrique's relative introduced a plan of action. "We need more information from the bank in Estockton," he said, giving the city its Spanish pronunciation. "We must know which local bank cashed the checks and who endorsed them."

The two cousins considered the situation in silence. Then Don Enrique addressed Bud.

"You could resolve this matter more quickly by traveling to Estockton yourself and meeting the bank officials face to face," he suggested.

"Absolutely not." Bud's tone was vehement. "No." And, without referring to his tax debt to the United States government, he rose abruptly and started pacing the floor. He said, "That's the last place I want to go," as if they had suggested Siberia or Mars. "I have too much to do at the Heights," he added.

This surprised Don Enrique, who for months had noticed an absence of buyers for the remaining properties on the hill at Amapolas.

Don Enrique tried again. He spoke of the value of meeting colleagues, of the danger of delays in the mail.

Bud shook his head. "Not me."

So a letter had to be drafted and mailed to the manager of the Stockton bank, which was located within a few miles of the groves where Altagracia's aunt's husband dug trenches, pruned and irrigated trees, and eventually picked from them thousands of bushels of nectarines, apricots, pears, and figs.

·········

THE MATTER OF the thefts became quickly
known in Amapolas, where, it was believed, the forger
would be apprehended. With their usual common sense,
the townspeople eliminated the post office as the possible
site of a crime. As long ago as anyone could remember,
Carmen's background was impeccable, and besides that,
her professional future was assured. Only high crime, made
public, could sever her from her position, which was lifelong, paid well, and gave her an opportunity to embroider,
knit, and tat as she chose.

Opinion in Amapolas pointed to an outsider, someone
who had access to mailbags and the chance to open secretly
envelopes bearing American stamps. One of the bus driv-
ers, for instance.

NOW, THE FORGERIES stopped and an ex-
change of letters between Bud and the bank in Stockton,
California, began in the drought of early June and ended
under an August downpour in the office of the bank president in La Luz. This gentleman, along with his cousin
Don Enrique Ortiz de León, had insisted that Bud Loomis,
because of his good name and excellent business reputation,
should act as correspondent between the banks.

And now, at last, two months later, it was done, the verification of names, dates, and addresses, of check numbers and sums of money, and finally the identification of the local financial institution that had accepted and cashed the forged checks.

"And which bank was it?" asked the banker.

"This one," Bud said.

Within a week's time, every member of the bank's staff, from the loan officer to the messenger, had been interrogated at least once. The president himself questioned the tellers, but to no end. Action came only when the executive board offered a bribe, or, as the president put it, a reward for information. This announcement led immediately, not to an arrest, but to a pair of disappearances. One was of a teller, a shy, soft-spoken employee named Virgilio, who immediately after the reward was offered left his station at Window Number Three and was never seen locally again.

The other abdication, sixty kilometers to the north, was noticed in Amapolas when, for the first time in village memory, the post office remained shuttered and locked until noon, when the mayor brought the Treviño brothers and a crowbar to force open the door.

As if she had never sat there, Carmen had left her counter clear of reminders. Gone were the needles, hooks, and bobbins, the shining loops of silk thread, the rainbow twists of wool. Gone the flasks of nail varnish in a dozen visceral shades.

By such evidence, the people of Amapolas pieced the affair together. They remembered Carmen's weekly visits to La Luz to turn in money and requisition stamps.

"Which of the two forged the checks?" the people of the village wondered. They said, "She is *sin vergüenza*, the shameless daughter of her weeping mother," and, "By now, the two of them have crossed the border." They would nod, supposing that Carmen and this Virgilio were already shopping for transistor radios, a washing machine, and even a Pontiac or Chevrolet.

Don Enrique, still regarded as *patrón* of Amapolas, arranged matters so that the vacant position of postmistress fell to Carmen's cousin Braulia, thus preserving the honor of the Ruiz line.

Meanwhile, anyone who looked could watch Ofelia's children fatten. For Don Enrique's second cousin, the bank president, not only repaid the stolen money in full but, along with the certified check, delivered a sack of cheeses and condensed milk to Ofelia's door.

NO ONE IN Amapolas had been surprised to discover in June that Altagracia was pregnant. A beautiful girl just turned sixteen in daily communication with a man inside a house that, in spite of new plans, still consisted of one large room—what else could one expect?

"Which parent will the child resemble?" the townspeople

asked each other. "Will it be Altagracia, with her long limbs and slender neck, or the shorter Señor Loomis?" They spoke of Bud as El Chaparro because of his height and remembered his square torso and thick arms and legs.

"The girl is *mestiza*," they remarked. "She is half Spanish, half Indian." They said, "The child will be half *mestizo*, half *gringo*."

During these first months, Altagracia walked about as straight and graceful as ever and, as always, merely by her passage, turned the heads of men.

Bud, for his part, made no acknowledgment of his approaching fatherhood. The enlargement of his house proceeded slowly, with Don Enrique's relative, the architect, in charge.

Everyone on the hill, including the two oldest, Herr Otto and Ursula Bowles, visited the building site to watch walls rise and pipes invade them. The house grew from one room with primitive plumbing to five served by both a tub and shower.

"It is easy to keep clean when you are rich," Patricio Gómez remarked to a friend. "You have hot water and can use as much soap and as many towels as you please."

Behind the emerging house, Bud's half acre of land lay untended, as innocent of care as on the day it was first encircled by a wall. Within this stone barrier topped with broken glass crowded a dozen varieties of cactus sheltered by a thicket of mesquite, so that, in the end, Bud's garden was entirely armed with thorns.

One September day, Sue Ames, expecting that Altagracia might clear a space, brought a present to this garden, a foot-high jacaranda in a can. She was knocking at the door when two men came up behind her. One was Don Enrique Ortiz de León, the other a stranger, a lean, lined American who looked tired. Don Enrique introduced this person as Señor Gray, pronouncing it "Grigh," as if it rhymed with *high*.

"An attorney like myself," he said. "We have mutual friends," and he named one in La Luz, one in Saltillo, and one in the national capital.

This is an exhausted man, Sue observed, shaking the stranger's hand.

Don Enrique, as though completing a résumé, continued, "Señor Grigh's client is the United States government, the tax department in particular." He glanced at his acquaintance. "He comes to Mexico from Arizona." This listing of credentials appeared to increase the fatigue of Robert Gray.

Aware of this, Sue said, "Let's sit," and led the two men to a bench.

Don Enrique had still more to explain. "Señor Grigh is about to retire," he said, "and I have invited him to consider one of the remaining properties here on our hill." He had lifted a hand to point in their direction when Bud Loomis appeared in his pickup and, producing billows of dust, drew up beside them. He jumped to the ground, pulling Altagracia out after him, and approached his visitors.

The next moment Bud was staring at Robert Gray, now risen from the bench. The visitor turned to stare at him.

Don Enrique began the introductions, but the three words "Señor Bud Loomis" were barely spoken when the American lawyer broke in. He said, "Bert Pratt, isn't it?"

Bud, facing the man who could convict and jail him, said, "How've you been?"

ONE AFTERNOON NOT long after this, Don Enrique sat at his desk under his grandmother's portrait and counseled his two American friends. He had already heard their separate accounts of the events of six years ago and was still puzzled that such a matter should prove difficult to resolve. He had discussed the charge of felony with Bud Loomis and learned that, as well as substantial fines, a prison sentence might be imposed.

"Why have you not offered a gift of some sort to Señor Grigh? A thank-you in advance for his cooperation?"

And Bud replied, "Because that would only lengthen my jail term."

Don Enrique was shocked. A prison sentence for the

exercise of common sense? For a simple resolution that required only good will and mutual understanding?

"How much do you owe?" Don Enrique asked, and shook his head at the answer. Then he said, "How much do you have?" and again shook his head.

Today, from across his desk, he regarded his client and the tax official into whose hands he had unwittingly delivered him. He understood that Bud, throughout his residence in Mexico, had used his mother's maiden name, instead of his father's surname, as his legal one. This did not astonish Don Enrique. The mother's unmarried name came last and always, at the end of every male Mexican's signature. In the case of his own name, Enrique César Ortiz de León, which rang with a certain bravura, Ortiz in the middle came from his father and de León at the end from his mother.

And now, Don Enrique, forgetting his visitors, sank into memory, his own and the one he had inherited. Ah, the tales that had been handed down of these de León! From the pool of hearsay, he fished up a great-great-aunt who had danced with Maximilian, and her brother who died fighting the French at Puebla.

A few seconds later, he had abandoned history and was addressing the two Americans.

"I find I must have more time to consider this matter. Today is Tuesday. Let us postpone further discussion until Thursday," and he shook hands with both men.

On Wednesday he talked alone with Bud. "Perhaps Señor Grigh will buy one of your lots," Don Enrique suggested. "In this way you would recover part of what you must pay."

Also on Wednesday, he invited the American attorney to lunch at the Posada del Sol, together with his cousin the banker. The two Mexican gentlemen spoke of Bud's pursuit of justice in the case of the hungry children, the respect he had gained in Amapolas. They mentioned his many small kindnesses to the people of the village, particularly to Altagracia Gómez and her family.

"I believe he is a changed man," Don Enrique said, and, still not completely understanding American tax law and its practice, added, "I believe he will meet you halfway."

Robert Gray, in spite of his position as guest and his *filete* and three glasses of red wine, lifted a hand to silence his host.

A few days later, with the matter still unresolved, Don Enrique took his new friend to Amapolas to visit the lake and the village and, once again, the mesa. Here Robert Gray was shown a vacant property. The tax attorney, tempted by the vivid quality of the air and the curious peace of the place, allowed himself a brief interval of impetuousness to consider the proposition. He was restored to clear thinking when he telephoned his wife in Arizona.

Mrs. Gray asked if he had lost his mind and said, "Live

in a place where you can't drink the water, eat the food, understand the exchange, or trust the police?"

In this way, she caused her husband to recover himself.

Soon after that, Robert Gray met his fellow countryman alone on the mesa. Altagracia, beating egg whites in a brown clay bowl, watched them from the door of Bud's augmented quarters.

The lawyer talked. Bud listened. With the expectant father before him, Altagracia, smooth as honey, in the doorway behind, and the air, clear as last night's rain, on his face, Robert Gray pronounced his judgment.

He said, "Once in a while I recommend clemency." He looked north and east and measured the hills. Then he said, "An installment now and a year to pay in full."

Bud said, "Thanks." He hesitated a moment. "There'll always be a place for you here on the mesa, if you change your mind." He paused again. "I can offer you a good deal on that lot against the hill."

"Watch it," said Robert Gray.

THE WEDDING OF Bert Pratt Loomis and Altagracia Gómez Sierra took place at the end of August in Don Enrique's rebuilt chapel, two months before the birth of their baby. Perhaps to honor the occasion, one rainstorm ended and the next held off, so that arriving guests walked past puddles that reflected sky.

Though the event gave the impression of a spontaneous happening, there had been preparations. Besides the sewing of satin and the stringing of beads, the solemnity of the occasion had been attested to by Bud's conferences with Padre Miguel. The obstinate American's willingness to expose himself to faith surprised everyone in the village and on the hill. The women of Amapolas understood that it was Altagracia's beauty that had brought him to his knees. Cynical men, seldom seen in church themselves, said, "Try to find him at mass three months from now." Patricio Gómez said, "Once converted, he will be the richest member of the parish. The padre will probably ask him to pay for a new roof."

On four separate occasions these people watched Bud enter the rectory and shook their heads. Inside, the priest struggled for Bud's soul. He recognized this opportunity as the greatest challenge he had ever faced, and all to be done in four hours.

"Ten hours of instruction is customary," he told his restless student, and Bud answered, "Four should do it."

So they sat four times for sixty minutes, while Padre Miguel strove to establish a three-way communication between Bud, himself, and God. These efforts, in spite of good will on the parts of all, failed. The priest could only listen while Bud quickly agreed to everything, in theory and practice.

This is not a spiritual man, the priest acknowledged to

himself. I can only count on his good nature, and he asked Bud to memorize three prayers.

In the end, Padre Miguel, reduced to a point of no compromise, said, "Can you promise me that the expected child, as well as future children of this marriage, will be raised as Catholics?"

Bud, already halfway to the door, turned. "*Sí, sí, sí,*" he told the priest impatiently, and followed this in English with "Hell, yes."

NOW, A WEEK later, the ceremony was about to begin. The widow Bowles, walking with uneven steps on Herr Otto's arm, entered the chapel first. She paused at the door to delight in the classic proportions of the narrow, high space and the gleaming antiquities with which Don Enrique had furnished the altar. Herr Otto, seating the widow on a bench near the front, proceeded to the ancient organ, a family heirloom, set against a plastered wall and soon was drawing from the yellowed keys a series of uncertain chords and headlong runs. A moment later he was attempting bars of Bach and Mendelssohn, and in five minutes had learned how to compensate for the occasional paralysis of a key or even a pedal.

Sue arrived next, her hair pushed up under a wide-brimmed hat, traces of paint on her hands. Frances Bowles followed soon after, bringing with her a stranger, a sandy-haired man who had an unkempt look and wore his raincoat throughout the ceremony.

Slowly achieving the modest length of the aisle came two respected natives of Amapolas, Don Enrique Ortiz de León and Pepe Gómez, his majordomo, ninety-three years old and leaning on the arm of his *patrón*. Don Enrique helped Pepe onto the front bench on the right, then, after bowing to the three North American ladies on the left, joined the quivering ancient, whose tremors were already causing the bench to shake.

Sue Ames pondered Pepe Gómez. She had never seen anyone so frail. Transparent with age, he was like a tissue-paper kite caught in a gale.

Next down the aisle came the doctor, followed by Don Enrique's secretary, Leni, and after her those who had been gathering outside. But when Altagracia's immediate family and her relatives on both sides had found seats, there was no more room in the chapel, and the overflow crowd waited on the stone path to see the bride enter.

Here, at the carved stone portal, her sisters and three cousins, wearing wildflowers in their hair, pressed around Altagracia, clinging to her lace sleeves and clutching at her satin skirt. Then they were inside, the children preceding her, cygnets before a swan. And finally, the bride, large and lovely with child, her hands full of white roses brought by Bud from La Luz. Herr Otto played "Traumerei" and "Für Elise."

Padre Miguel, standing at the altar with Bud, restless and flushed beside him, forgot his misgivings about the sanctity of the chapel, which had yet to be blessed by the bishop, and about the religious convictions of the groom. This union can only be God's will, he told himself.

Sue, looking across the aisle, saw that Leni held a notepad and a pencil. But is she getting it all down? Sue wondered. Has she put down the wild cosmos in a copper bowl beside the altar? The quivering Pepe and the three fattening little girls? Altagracia's mother has begun to weep. Herr Otto has tricked the old organ into pure melody and is playing "Sheep May Safely Graze." Across the aisle from the secretary, the three North American women, aged thirty-two, forty-two, and eighty-three, sit, each alone, trying to remember love. Leni, have you put it all down?

Exit
the
Widow

....

SUCH A MONTH for dying it was, that December of 1967. Not only had two newborn infants been lost to defective hearts and the Monteros' teen-age son to an accident on a borrowed motorcycle, but the mayor's six-year-old niece was struck and killed in the plaza by a bus that backed over her. Besides these premature fatalities, four elders breathed their last. One of them was old Cruz López, who died of alcohol poisoning, and one was old Rosa Castillo, who stepped barefoot on a rusty nail. The two others were Pepe Gómez, Don Enrique's ancient retainer, and, at year's end in her house on the mesa, the widow Bowles.

Weeks before consulting the latest intern in Amapolas,

Ursula Bowles came to realize that, at last, she was coming into her inheritance. By the time that the *practicante*, Dr. Mario Sainz, confirmed her suspicions as to the nature of her symptoms, she had already assumed that the family legacy was now hers, handed down by her grandmother, her mother, and two aunts.

"You must go to La Luz for tests," Dr. Sainz said.

Ursula, facing this intern who was beginning his two-year term of government service, believed he was the youngest doctor so far to be stationed in Amapolas. When the widow asked his age and he said he was twenty-five, she continued to search his face for signs of a beard.

"I entered the university at eighteen and medical school at twenty-one," he told her. "And have had a year's experience at the hospital in La Luz."

"In which part of the city is that?" she asked, and, as he explained what street the hospital faced, resolved never to go there.

"I will refer you to a specialist on the hospital staff," the intern said, and it was then the widow Bowles started saying, "No," though she would eventually see this specialist on occasion.

After their first talk, Ursula visited the intern again in his clinic that faced the village square. "I have selected you to be my doctor," she told him. "I place myself in your hands."

"WOULD YOU LIKE to go back to New Mex-
ico?" Fran Bowles asked her mother. "We could rent something, perhaps in the mountains. Of course, I'd stay with
you."

"I think I want to die here," the widow said, and, with
the wave of an arm, she gathered to her the dozen square
sections of the world framed by her windows.

Sue Ames, from the second house down the road, started to
pay daily visits. On one polished October afternoon, she crayoned a quick portrait of Ursula sitting in her garden between
a pomegranate tree in a tub and two potted white geraniums.

When Sue showed her subject the drawing, the widow
said, "So that is how I look, like a survivor." She held the
picture as if it, not she, could claim to be Ursula Bowles,
understanding, of course, that within a few months this
would be the case.

Even before the intern suggested to Ursula that she was
dying, she had started to empty shelves and drawers. "What
is this?" she would ask herself, holding up a silver brocade
scarf. "Why did I bring it to Mexico?" Or in the case of
a brass paperweight in the shape of a woman's ringed hand,
"Why this?"

Ursula was specific about a few bequests.

"Please give everything in the kitchen cupboards to Trinidad Gómez and Ofelia." Then, glancing at a table against

the wall, she said, "I'd like that to go to Padre Miguel," and pointed to the portable record player and the dozen symphonies and concertos piled beside it.

"Does he like music?" her daughter asked, and Ursula said, "Probably."

The widow's disposal of her possessions continued for the rest of her life, a period of approximately six months. It seemed that she had accumulated and brought with her to Amapolas more spoons and glasses, more bookmarks and pens than anyone in the town or on the hill could have imagined.

In this way, Ursula's house was cleared of many objects before, instead of after, her death.

AT THE SAME time, in his house at Revolution Street Number 10, Pepe Gómez, too, was dying. He had been born on the matrimonial bed in a room of this house almost a century ago. In those days, the lake, the painted pink and yellow houses that were sometimes reflected in it, the plaza, the *hacienda* on the mesa above, and the thousand *hectáreas* of land around it all had belonged to the family Ortiz de León. If Pancho Villa had not galloped through at the head of his ragtag band of recruits, impulsive with pistols and dry-throated for *pulque*, the serene old life of a few rich and a multitude of poor might have endured.

Pepe, wrapped in a weathered *sarape*, sitting in the sun at the door of the adobe house his grandfather built with his own hands, could remember Villa's liberation of Amapolas. Behind Pepe there stretched a lifetime of Novembers, loud on the twentieth day with parades, band music, fireworks, and speeches. Pepe was no different from the next man. He, too, liked to eat and keep a solid roof over his family. But at this moment, he believed that all he wanted was to serve an Ortiz or a de León again. Any one of them, he now told himself, father, son, grandson. He would have reversed time if he could, not for even greater political freedom, but in order to answer bells, wait at massive doorways, carry silver trays down mazes of high-ceilinged halls.

IN THESE FIRST weeks of her last illness, Ursula Bowles began a closer inspection of the village of Amapolas than she had ever given it before.

"May I have a lift?" she would say to her daughter Frances or to Sue Ames, when she saw one of them backing her car into the lane. Then the two women would cross the mesa between Don Enrique's remodeled birthplace and the new whitewashed adobe dwellings that it overshadowed. Once in the village, the widow, after the purchase of a mango or a melon and a few stamps, would sit in the plaza on the bench that faced the church steps and observe fifteen minutes of life being lived in a hamlet of a thousand souls.

It was the old and the children who were drawn to sit beside her or stand in front of her and stare. Ursula attempted conversations with them all.

"Were you born in Amapolas? Is your house nearby?" she would ask. Or, "What is the name of the tree with the yellow flowers?" Or, pointing to an emaciated dog, lying listless under the bench, "I wonder if this animal is yours?"

At first, silence greeted these advances, but when the presence of the widow, usually wearing a denim skirt and a red sweater, became ordinary and expected, exchanges of talk naturally followed.

"I am eighty-three years old," Ursula replied to a question from a stooped, wrinkled woman, whose smile disclosed bare gums. "You and I must be almost the same age." And she remarked to herself, I am the lucky one. I have all my teeth.

The children would point down one of the narrow cobbled lanes that converged on the plaza and say, "That is my house with the birdcage on the wall," or, "Do you see the woman with the *olla* on her head? That is my mother. She is carrying home water from the lake."

Ursula would look in the dusty, weedy directions of these things and nod. She was concerned, as well, about the homes and fortunes of the mongrels she regularly noticed snapping and scuffling among the calla lilies in the square behind her.

"Does someone regularly feed these dogs?" the widow asked her new acquaintances, who first stared at her in surprise, then said, "¿*Sabe?*"

From the time of her first visit to this bench in the plaza, Ursula had noticed how many more women than men climbed the steps to enter the church. Is our sex the spiritual one, she asked herself, and males in general skeptical? The widow pondered the matter and one afternoon, perhaps hoping for an answer, went inside and sat down on a bench at the rear.

Believing herself to be alone, she spoke out loud. "Why, it's lovely," she said. "All this azure-blue and gold." And, as her voice filled the freshly painted nave, two shawled heads turned back from a front bench to observe her. She understood that these women attributed her raised voice, as well as her lack of piety, to the fact that she was North American and had been raised outside the Church. Ursula had to control an impulse to walk down the aisle and join these worshipers.

"I also believe in considering life and death," she longed to tell them. "They are tremendous things. The problem is to make them fit." Ursula looked across the rows of empty pews toward the pair of heads bowed before the altar. "I also keep wishing," she wanted to tell them. She wanted to say, "We are the same. I am like you."

As Ursula stepped out into the September sunlight, she came face to face with Padre Miguel hurrying from the street to the church door. The padre made no effort to conceal his surprise.

"Señora," he said. "Welcome." He smiled.

A month later, after the widow's condition had become generally known in Amapolas, the priest approached Ursula on her bench outside the church one morning and said, "Señora, I want you to know that I pray for you daily."

"Oh, please don't," Ursula started to say, but at the last minute, fearing to be rude, she left off the *don't*, and Padre Miguel heard her respond, "Oh, please."

Because of this misunderstanding, the widow was forced to live the rest of her life with the knowledge that unauthorized supplications were regularly being offered up on her behalf.

AT THIS TIME, the widow's daughter Fran was dividing her time between Amapolas and the jungles of Yucatán.

"Change no plans on my account," the widow told her. "Go ahead with your research. Then come back and tell me about it."

So Fran Bowles came and went during those autumn months, spending a week or two on the central plateau and a week or two in the tropics. Each time she returned to the mesa above Amapolas, she noticed the gradual chilling of the evenings and the need for a sweater in the noontime shade. The jungle, on the other hand, never changed. On every visit, moisture that was almost visible hung in the air, causing fibrous green leaves to drip. Vines clawed their way up Indian ceremonial columns designed to point straight to the sun at high noon and the full moon at midnight.

"How far along are you with the book?" Ursula would ask, and Frances would answer, "Still halfway. I'm waiting for Carter Riley's latest archaeological report."

The widow did not say, "Who is Carter Riley? Where did you meet? Are you in love?" Instead, she reverted, as she often did these days, to the uncontroversial question of what to do with what she called "the rest of my things." These included a few pieces of jewelry, a beaded bag and a pair of opera glasses from her grandmother, her mother's steamer trunk, still labeled, two boxes of letters and one of photographs.

Frances responded, as always, "Oh, don't let's think of it now," but her mother persisted.

"This house," she said, turning to look around her at its white walls, tiled floor, and shuttered windows. "I want to give it to you."

Her daughter protested. "But I have one almost exactly like it next door."

Ursula saw reason in this and, knowing Frances could live comfortably without adding these rooms and the walled garden around them to her assets, considered an alternative solution. She fell silent, listing in her mind possible alternatives. In the end, she discarded them all. Padre Miguel lived by tradition behind the church, and the intern at the back of the clinic. The schoolmaster rented two rooms from the mayor and had his eye on a future in politics.

"I believe I will leave this house to Clara Daggett," the widow said without warning.

"Do you mean your old school friend?" Frances stared at her mother. "Isn't she your age and in one of those final places?"

"Yes," Ursula said. "She does live in one of those places, but I can tell from her letters that she hasn't lost her mind."

For her part, Frances declared that the whole idea was insane. "Clara Daggett can't even get to Amapolas, much less live here."

"You are right, of course." Now Ursula rose and crossed her *sala* to the window that faced east. "She discovered Mexico when she discovered me, in the seventh grade, and I told her how astonishing this country is. I realize she will never actually come here." Then Ursula turned back to Frances. "But don't you see? If she has my house for a year or two, this particular piece of Mexico will be hers. Actually hers to imagine, and therefore even touch, even see. Whether or not she ever comes."

The widow watched her daughter stand and pull on a

sweater. "Haven't I told you all this? About first meeting Clara Daggett?"

"Yes, of course," Frances said, controlling her impatience. "But how will the house be disposed of in the end?" And it was clear she believed that, as soon as Clara died, the structure in which daughter and mother now conversed would be drawn into a permanent vacuum, to exist eternally as an unsolved problem.

"It will be this way," the widow told her daughter. "Clara will leave instructions for the house to be sold when she dies and for the proceeds given to a project."

"What one?" Frances asked, more out of curiosity than disapproval.

"I have no idea," Ursula said, although by evening, imagination serving as it does, she would have the answer.

Wrapped in her oldest fringed shawl, her chair drawn close to a mesquite-branch fire, Ursula reached into a long-undisturbed layer of her past and dragged to the surface her first day in the seventh grade in a California school.

At that time she was a displaced child, removed against her will from a Mexican mining town, each of whose steep streets, tracked by burros and canaled by rains, were better known to her than the lines on the palms of her own twelve-year-old hands. The houses that fronted these lanes were painted at the base with a wide band of color, hard yellow, soft blue, shrimp pink, all of them pocked by a kicking hoof, a thrown stone, or the blade of a plow. From a vast distance, the dying Ursula now dragged into her view the wilted plaza that served these dwellings. The dwarfed trees in the town square clearly longed for richer soil, the drooping calla lilies for deeper shade. For a few seconds the widow Bowles, sitting momentarily without discomfort before her fire at Amapolas, wanted nothing more in life than to walk along the cracked brick paths of this plaza, between the benches where worn old men and women rested. They said, *"Buenos días, niña,"* and she said *"Buenos días"* back, until she had passed them all.

At the foot of the mountain that, according to engineers, was riddled with rich veins of silver ore, a convent had been built a century or so ago. Once located on the broad estate of an *hacendado*, it now found itself, without moving its walls a centimeter, on a lane among farms.

Here six sisters of the Order of the Sacred Heart taught local women how to sew and children how to read and write. When she was seven years old, Ursula, after learning letters and numbers with her mother for a year, was enrolled in the nuns' school.

Under the scrutiny of these gentle perfectionists, Ursula, her hair in braids and ribbons, learned to spell, recite, and understand long division. She was given homework, which made the ascent in a saddlebag while she looked at the view from Rosi's back.

For the next five years, except during vacations and in torrential rains, Ursula, riding her placid horse, Rosi, and followed by the gardener, Manuel, on his friskier one, took the road that wound steeply down from the manager's house at the mine to the tree-shaded convent a mile below. Then Manuel led Rosi up the mountain, and the three returned to take Ursula home in the afternoon.

Sometimes Ursula took out her scratch pad and pencil and practiced writing her name while Rosi picked the easiest way up the slope. Then she would hand these things to Manuel and tell him to sign his own.

"*Fijate, niña,*" he would say. "Imagine it. I cannot write."

Then they would stop for a minute on the road and she would show him how.

"Divide six by two," she would say, and when Manuel shook his head, she would search the saddlebag, discover half a dozen sugared nuts the nuns had given her, and pass three to him. Silently, they would eat these nuts.

In this way they learned together.

But at the end of five years, for reasons never made clear to her, Ursula heard talk of travel, watched trunks pulled from storerooms, and found herself included in a general exodus. One morning the child Ursula, loudly protesting, was dragged from Mexico, clinging, as she thought she remembered, to doorknobs and gates, clutching at stone walls and tree branches, shouting, "No! No!" to the deaf world around her.

Within a few months she entered school in San Francisco.

Here, torn from the tutelage of the nuns, an alien in a class of her peers, Ursula floundered among square roots and the hypotenuses of triangles. Twice, after class, she ran to the cloakroom to weep.

It was in this airless spot, on the second occasion, that Clara Daggett discovered her. Without wasting time on clean handkerchiefs and sympathy, Clara said, "It is easier than you think," and left the room.

Two weeks passed before the morning when Ursula, red-faced at her desk, tried to compute the speed of the current of a stream from a canoe as she floated, watch in hand, past two pine trees one hundred feet apart. The young Ursula allowed herself to be swept past the trees a dozen times before she surrendered and laid down her pencil in defeat.

Clara Daggett was waiting at the classroom door. She asked, "Did you get the miles per hour?" Then, without pausing for an answer, she pointed to a bench facing the playground. "I'll meet you there at recess," Clara said, and thus, in regular ten-minute sessions, transformed panic into common sense. In return, Ursula explained Mexico to her new friend. Later, and for the rest of her life, Ursula had followed Clara's career through school bulletins. Professorships, degrees, and honors had all been hers. Suddenly Ursula, shawled and almost completely without pain in her house in Mexico, saw, as in a vision, Clara Daggett establishing a teaching program devoted to straightening out the minds of all the twelve-year-olds who drifted down rivers between trees, who knows how fast.

Ursula reminded herself to inform Frances of this solution to the problem of the bequest. Now, the matter finally resolved, the widow rose and broke her fire's last coals into ashes. Clara Daggett, though disposed of, continued to make her presence felt. Ursula lingered in her *sala* to compare the interior of her own mind with Clara's. Here she was, the widow Bowles, nearly at the end of her life, and her thoughts still not in order. By now, I should have more answers and be able to prove them. She knew that even now, at eighty-three, if she could see inside her head, she would find disarray. She would discover thoughts in embryo, projects only dreamed of, backward looks she had meant to take, words she had put together and never spoken.

On the other hand, when Ursula imagined Clara Daggett's mind, she saw perfect order. Inside Clara's head a serenity that was almost architectural ruled. It was a spacious, columned place, like the Jefferson Memorial, Ursula thought, or a Palladian villa outside Venice.

ONE LATE AFTERNOON in November, as the widow Bowles sat in her accustomed place at one side of the square, she heard slow footsteps on her right and turned to see Patricio Gómez and his great-grandfather approaching. A moment later, Don Pepe was sitting at her side.

What can these two ancients have to say to each other? Patricio asked himself, and he moved a short distance away to listen behind their backs.

The widow began the conversation with a foolish question. "How is your health?" she asked.

Pepe answered by giving her a date, "I was born September 16th, one thousand, eight hundred, seventy-four or -five."

"Independence Day," Ursula said, happy to stumble on an annual celebration to which the old man could be anchored. "I remember the parades and speeches when I lived in Mexico as a child."

But old Pepe had stopped listening after the words "I remember," and was asleep in the sun.

Not noticing his closed eyes, the widow continued to impart information, about a mine two hundred kilometers from here, about the house on a hill where she was born, her teachers, who were nuns.

At this moment, Padre Miguel emerged from the church, descended the worn front steps, and approached the bench where Ursula and Pepe sat.

Two elderly residents of this community, and both almost totally unknown to me, he said to himself. Though, in both cases, their absence from mass is understandable, he went on silently. Since the priest's arrival in Amapolas six years ago, he had yet to hear a confession from Don Pepe Gómez. But what sins could a man of such an age have committed and still remember? the priest asked himself.

As for the North American widow, her faith defied analysis. She appeared to be a nonbeliever and glad of it, yet she had entered the church a month ago and, without a prayer, sat there for an hour.

He addressed her now, looking into her face, which was shaded by the wide brim of her hat.

He said, "Señora, will you come inside to rest?" and, because of the low level of his expectations, was scarcely surprised at her response.

"Oh, thanks, but not today," she said. "At the moment, I'm too tired to think." And, as she spoke these words, glanced up the street, where the intern now closed the clinic door behind him and approached her. Like the priest, he bent to look into her face. Then he turned without speaking and retraced his steps to the clinic, and again back to her. This time he carried a cup of water and two pills in a bottle.

"Take one now and one tonight," he told her. "I will come to see you tomorrow evening."

Such was the influence of Dr. Mario Sainz, one-year intern at the hospital in La Luz and two-year director of public health in the village of Amapolas, that Ursula Bowles, feeling an onset of the vigor that used to be hers, rose all at once to her feet and was giving Patricio instructions when Sue Ames appeared in her car to drive her home.

Patricio watched as Ursula Bowles arranged, in English, to borrow this car in a day or two so that he could drive her a few hundred kilometers east of here, to pay a last visit to her birthplace, a mine named Bolsas de Plata by its Spanish explorers because of its buried pockets of silver.

"Of course. Take the car," Sue Ames said.

Patricio, understanding only a few words of this conversation, accurately foresaw the details of this enterprise. He detected in advance the wrong roads they would take, the dusty detours, the futile interrogations of farmers in their fields, the misuse of time.

Now he was helping the widow Bowles into Sue's station wagon.

"Which day and what hour?" he asked, and when the widow said, "Wednesday at eight o'clock sharp," he nodded.

THE MORNING OF the drive to the Bolsas de Plata mine dawned cold and clear. No sooner had they descended the mesa than the widow began pointing out the yellowing leaves of cottonwoods, trees with which Patricio had spent all his life of twenty years. He had nothing to say about their overnight transformation. Instead, he asked for instructions about the route they were to take.

"Señora," he said, "have you brought a map?"

At this, Ursula Bowles said, "Of course," and produced one marked along its width in red crayon.

"Here we are now," she said, and, finding it with some difficulty, pointed to the spot where they had paused at the edge of the paved road that ran past the outskirts of Amapolas.

"So we are to turn right."

"Ordinarily, yes," the widow said. "But I must stop at the bank in La Luz before going on to the mine."

She asked Patricio to stop and, side by side on the front seat, they studied the map.

"The bank is not on the way," Patricio remarked. "Going there will cause us to drive an additional hundred kilometers." He folded the map. "At least."

"I must cash a check," Ursula Bowles told him, and at this, he glanced sidelong at his passenger. Perhaps she means to shop at fruit stands along the road, though it is not the season, he told himself, or to drink from a healing spring she may have heard about. As for her birthplace, this Bolsas de Plata mine, he could imagine no need for cash there, especially as he had no expectation of being able to find the place.

At the bank in La Luz, Ursula refused Patricio's offer of help. "Wait for me here," she said. "Have a Pepsi or a Coca."

Inside the bank she waited in the crowd of people push-

ing toward *Cambios* until the teller noticed her and took
her check.

"For cash," she said. "In clean thousand-peso bills."

The teller looked at the check and looked at the widow.
Seeing that she was North American and old, he converted
the peso total into dollars for her information. He examined
her face. Both old and failing, he now saw.

"This check is for more than a thousand dollars in your
money," he informed her, and the widow said, "Are there
not sufficient funds in my account?"

So in the end the teller handed the widow an envelope
of cash and then watched her leave the bank, holding her
hand to her eyes against the light at the door, feeling with
her shoe for steps.

It is a deposit for her funeral, he told himself later, and
he thought, What a casket!

Patricio, waiting outside, had examined the map and now
said he knew a shortcut that would eliminate almost any
retracing of the way they had already come.

But they were only thirty kilometers from La Luz when
the dirt road they were traveling reached a dead end. Twice
more that morning, in spite of Patricio's resourceful discovery of new roads, the widow and her driver watched
them end in a pasture or canal.

"If we are heading north, we must look for mountains
to our left," Ursula Bowles said, raising this landmark out
of the depths of her forgetting.

"Over there," and Patricio pointed to some hills and headed cross-country in their direction.

It was here on this plain, approaching these hills, that Ursula realized her energy was spent. This is the last daring excursion I shall take, she told herself, and sent her thanks skyward, perhaps to an assembly of saints and angels, perhaps to a flock of noisy crows making its way from one winter field to another.

Now, at the foot of the hills, they were nearing a cluster of pepper trees and the rubble of what were formerly adobe walls. The widow recognized these at once as the remains of the nuns' school.

"Stop here," she said, and was out of the car before Patricio could offer his hand. Now she was turning over a tile with her foot.

Patricio found three carved stones and set them in a row to form a lily on a stem. He found another with a word chiseled into it.

GLORIA, the stone said, and Ursula examined the rubble again, as if she expected it to produce music or a lighted candle.

"We are very close to the mine I am looking for," she said.

And when they turned, there it was, no more than a kilometer away, a rise that started gradually, then climbed sharply to a peak, the headframe of a shaft near the top.

Below it roofless buildings and rusty iron sheds tilted in decay.

A few minutes later, the old woman and her escort had arrived at the foot of the mountain, where a gate topped with barbed wire prevented entrance from the road. NO HAY PASO, read the sign, its letters partially dissolved by rains.

Ursula noticed a cluster of adobe huts outside the fence. From one of these emerged a man whose felt hat and gun and toothpick marked him as an official. Ursula saw immediately there was a resemblance between this man and her dimming recollection of the patient Manuel, who had escorted her on school days down the mountain to the nuns and, later on, taken her home again.

Soon fifteen or twenty people stood about, caretakers, it seemed, all living here with wives and children in this world that existed by itself, an island in space.

The widow found her voice and stated her purpose. She said she was born in the house at the top of the mountain and pointed in the direction where her birthplace might or might not yet be found.

"I am looking for Manuel Diaz," the widow said, forgetting that he would be a man of 106 by now.

Without hesitation, a stooped and wrinkled man stepped forward and said, "I am his grandson," and eight others advanced to introduce themselves as great-nephews and great-grandsons.

"May I speak to you?" the widow asked, and under the eyes of all who were gathered there, including the armed guard from company headquarters in Parral, and including Patricio Gómez, Ursula Bowles said, "I was happy here as a child. Your relative was a kind friend," and opened her purse.

When Patricio saw her take out the bills, he commented, *Una loca*, to himself, then approached, and when he saw that each bill had a value of a thousand pesos, he spoke. Taking her arm and turning away from the others, he tried to counsel her.

"*Mire, señora*," he said. "Look. These people may very well be robbing you. They have shown no proof that they are related to this man you remember, this Manuel Diaz."

The widow made no reply. An obstinate look hardened her glance. Without acknowledging Patricio's recommendation of caution, she allowed her eyes to rest briefly on the bearded shadow of a man in torn overalls before handing him his gift.

Patricio, his back to the crowd, addressed her with quiet urgency. "Señora, stop to reflect. You are probably filling the pockets of thieves and no-accounts with riches they in no way deserve. Señora, think of this for a moment."

But the widow Bowles ignored him, turned back, and handed bills to eight or nine others in the group around her. At last, making her way across the compound, she arrived at the side of a barefoot woman hung with small children from her *rebozo* to her layered skirts.

Ursula Bowles asked a question. "Is your family name Diaz?" she said, and the woman nodded, as she probably would have done had Ursula asked if her father was a Robles, Sánchez, Rodríguez, or Durón.

"Then I want you to have this," and the widow pushed the last thousand-peso bill into a fold of the shawl that swaddled the baby. "I knew your great-grandfather when I was your age," she said, looking down at a little girl, who stared back silent beneath the massed tangle of her hair.

"That is, if your age is seven," Ursula went on to the child. "I rode down the mountain to be taught by the nuns. I rode a horse named Rosi."

After this, there was nothing more to be said, and Patricio helped the widow into the car. The drive home, to the west, took three hours, with the sun in their eyes all the way.

THIS TRIP, APPROVED neither by the intern nor by Frances Bowles, proved to be ill-advised. It depleted the widow's hoarded energy to the extent that after that day she seldom left her house. Friends, bringing covered plates of food designed to tempt, stayed for only a few minutes of one-sided conversation and left as if by request.

In this way three weeks passed. The intern visited every day. Fran Bowles canceled a proposed short trip to Yucatán. Sue Ames, stricken to realize how little she could do to help, postponed her annual winter stay in San Miguel. From the village of Amapolas came herbs and instructions for their use, came the siftings of the advice of *brujos*, the proved cures, the supplications to ancient gods. Padre Miguel called on the widow twice a week and showed himself to be a man of unusual chivalry and tact by postponing his prayers for her soul until he was outside her door.

On a warm December morning, enjoying an hour of comparative well-being, Ursula reminded her daughter, Fran, of the status of final arrangements that she herself had made.

Together they went over the will. Her mother, Fran saw, had remembered every man, woman, and child who had ever worked for her—the tree pruner, the seamstress, Fran's piano teacher.

"Are these addresses still correct?" the widow's daughter asked her mother, who, unconcerned, replied, "As far as I know," and went on, "Don't worry about Clara Daggett posing problems. Her inheritance of this house will work itself out."

Fran said, "Of course."

"And don't worry about my ashes," Ursula went on. "The undertakers in La Luz, Gallegos Brothers, will hold them until you, or someone, goes to New Mexico. To the Sangre de Cristo Mountains, near the ranch."

Fran said, "Of course."

The two women sat for a moment without speaking, side by side on the sofa facing the fire. All at once, Ursula Bowles stretched out her right hand to lie for a moment on the folded hands of her daughter. The widow knew these hands so well that she could recognize their earlier stages in them now. With her hand quiet on Fran's, she could have accurately traced their shape and size at any given date from her child's infancy until now.

ONE EVENING NOT long before the widow Bowles died, five people gathered by coincidence in her *sala*. Present were Don Enrique, who had brought a bottle of fine wine, the intern, who had come to give his patient an injection, Padre Miguel, on one of his regular visits, Sue Ames, and Fran.

"Rest in bed," Dr. Mario Sainz advised Ursula, and he left her door into the *sala* open.

Ursula Bowles, half lying, half sitting against three pillows in her bed, with flowers from Sue's garden and an untouched glass of Don Enrique's wine on the table beside her, listened to the quiet talk in the next room. At first, one or another of the group would come to her door every few minutes with bits of conversation in an effort to include her. When she closed her eyes, they assumed she was asleep and, after that, left her undisturbed.

It was now that Ursula, nearing the end of her days, discovered at last what life is. She could hear the voices but not the words of her guests. They spoke in shallow waves that rose and broke, subsided, and rose again. Occasionally, someone laughed. Frances had lit two lamps, and as people moved about, their shadows came and went on Ursula's bedroom wall. She found herself enjoying this silent company.

Our lives are brief beyond our comprehension or our desire, she told herself. We drop like cottonwood leaves from trees after a single frost. The interval between birth and death is scarcely more than a breathing space. Tonight, in her house on a Mexican hill, Ursula Bowles listened to the five assembled in her *sala* and thought she heard the faint rustle of their days slipping by. She could see now that an individual life is, in the end, nothing more than a stirring of air, a shifting of light. No one of us, finally, can be more than that. Even Einstein. Even Brahms.

Then the widow slept.

The
Bandstand
in the Square

....

THAT WEEK IN August began much like any other. On Monday, the mason's son, jailed after midnight Sunday on a drunk-and-disorderly charge, successfully dug his way through the adobe wall of his cell before morning, using only his fingernails and a belt buckle, to emerge into open air as the sun came up. Before noon on Tuesday, because of an unseasonable drought and in spite of government guarantees, the new water pump failed and the village well ran dry.

On Tuesday night, the mayor, considered by all to be a good man, drove with his mistress to a cantina in a town forty miles east of Amapolas and, on the way home, while the car was stopped off the road for a few moments, accidentally shot her as they embraced in the front seat. Although her wound was minor, the event was destined to end in tragedy.

All day Wednesday, the women of the village waded past cows into the shrinking lake to fill their jars and buckets and lift them to their heads. In this way they carried their drinking water home. By noon, it became known to the townspeople that the mayor's mistress had died, but not because of the bullet wound in her thigh. The fact was that she bled to death on the way to the hospital in La Luz, located as it was so far from the scene of the accident. Now what would become of the mayor, so well-liked by everyone? His wife hid behind closed shutters and kept the children home.

On Thursday, Dr. Mario Sainz, the intern, addressed a poorly attended conference of children's mothers at the clinic. "Boil milk," he instructed them. "Boil water."

On the same day and all day Friday, Blas Arriaga, twenty-three years old and hotheaded, went on a hunger strike outside the mayor's office to protest the governor's lack of concern in the matter of the pump and well.

"This state official has no understanding of the situation," Blas argued to passersby. "His mother and sister, unlike ours, need not carry water to their houses from the lake." In spite of the absence of the mayor, who had been taken into custody by the authorities in La Luz, Blas stayed at his post one day, one night, and half another day without food or water as far as anyone could see.

The doctor watched the protest from the door of the clinic Friday morning, mentally reviewing the weekly report he must present to his superior in the city. A full month had passed since the afternoon he stood in the street, looked up, saw a finger pointing out of a cloud at Amapolas, and heard a voice command, "Let there be dysentery."

"Two infants dead," he would have to write. "Two critical," he would have to add. "Another dozen children at grave risk."

Dr. Sainz gazed at the recently constructed bandstand in the plaza as if its inauguration on Sunday might produce solutions instead of song.

Ay, ay, ay, ay, a voice wailed inside the intern. *Cantas no lloras.*

The
Bandstand
in the
Square
....
197

SUE AMES, SITTING on her terrace wall late that Friday afternoon, gazed down on the square below and mourned. She mourned all living things without distinction, the mayor in his plight and the children struck down by dysentery, the thirsty cattle in the fields, as well as their helpless masters, and went on to include the donkey beaten about the head with sticks, and the straggle-bearded derelict she saw yesterday asleep at the broken curb.

At this moment Patricio Gómez appeared from behind the house and approached to stand beside her.

His glance followed hers to the village plaza. "Bad news," he said. "There is little hope that the *kiosco* will be finished by Sunday afternoon," and he pointed in the general direction of the new bandstand in the square.

"It will have to be finished," Sue said, and turned to face him. "It cannot not be finished."

Patricio, watching Sue's mouth and eyes turn obstinate, lost himself in reflection. Of the three North American señoras who had come here, the one who died, the one often absent in Yucatán, and the woman before him now, he had from the beginning considered this one the most beautiful. The most beautiful and the most foolish.

"A section of the balustrade is missing," he told her, "and the wrought iron still has to be painted." Keeping his eyes on her face, he continued, "Without that work done, it is impossible to plant the bougainvillea vines you selected."

At this, Sue rose and they stood together in silence at the mesa's edge, contemplating the new bandstand. It was obvious, even from a distance, even in its unfinished state, that the small structure was perfect in its proportions and design. Sue perceived it at this moment as clear evidence of life's random grace and was briefly cheered.

"I will be in the plaza at eight o'clock tomorrow morning

to speak to the foreman of the job," she said. "Unless the Señora Francisca returns tonight from the tropics to take charge. As the widow's daughter, it is she who must be satisfied."

But this is not actually true, Sue told herself. The one person to please is Ursula herself, now eight months dead. And suddenly Sue, as though she believed in eternal life, saw the widow sitting on a bench in front of the kiosk, admiring its octagonal shape, the iron grapes and leaves that rose in columns of filigree to support its iron roof, the raised tile floor, smooth enough for dancing, the circling balustrade against which a small orchestra could play—all things Ursula herself might have chosen. Sue stood on her terrace, convinced that Fran Bowles, so often wrong, had been right this time, to give the village a bandstand in memory of her mother. As the sun sank behind Sue's house and evening came on, a hush fell on the square.

"What about the mariachi band?" Sue asked Patricio, and he quickly reassured her.

"Señora, the matter is in hand. If I may use your car tomorrow, I will drive to La Luz and make arrangements with a *conjunto* in one of the cantinas." He paused to think. "In La Vida Nueva or, perhaps, La Hora de Oro."

"Once I drove past a cantina in La Luz called Recuerdos del Porvenir," Sue said, and Patricio nodded.

"I will visit that one, too." Then he waved, stepped

on the parapet, dropped out of sight, and a moment later could be heard slipping and sliding down the face of the bluff.

Sue continued to sit on the wall. What could it mean, the name of that bar? Memories of the Future. Or, perhaps, Recollections of What Is to Come. Possibly, one must be drunk to understand it. But here, outside in the still air of evening, she felt herself on the verge of solving the riddle. Months, or was it years ago, sudden images of her former husband's eyes, his chin, and hands had begun to invade her tranquility. More and more frequently, against her will and against all caution, she had found herself summoning up Tim's uncompromising glance, his rare and unpredictable laugh.

"Let me know if you need anything. Tell me what," he had written in a letter she never answered. Now, swayed by an uncharacteristic sense of helplessness, she found herself wishing him here—just until Fran Bowles gets back, she told herself. Just to see that the bandstand is finished. And one more thing he could do if he came, take charge of Ursula's ashes.

It was almost too dark by now to see the wooden cross that marked the site of these ashes in the graveyard below, at the far southeast corner, where the wall had broken into rubble. Here it was impossible to tell the difference between holy and ordinary ground or to determine on which side of the boundary Ursula's remains had been mistakenly interred. The demarcation of the cemetery's limits was further blurred at this point by a hardy morning glory that had spread rampant over all of this grave and sections of two others. Buried in a copper box under this azure sprawl lay Ursula's ashes, consigned in error to the adobe soil of the *panteón* in Amapolas instead of to the wind that gusted up the slope of a mountain in New Mexico. I am not responsible, Sue tried to convince herself. Fran Bowles will have to take care of it. Tim is not here.

The sky was still faintly red with sunset an hour later, when Sue turned to enter her house. Sounds of activity rose from the plaza. She heard shouts of children, howls of dogs, the grinding of the bus's gears, and, before she closed her door, the first notes of a trumpet fanfare.

IN THE KITCHEN, where Sue ate meatball soup and rewarmed tortillas that night, a thick white paper map of the world covered one wall. This was a joint project, executed by herself and the three Gómez sisters, who appeared together or singly every morning to wash her dishes and dust her table and chairs. When their work was done and time still left before noon and lunch, the aproned girls, now ten, twelve, and fourteen years old, climbed footstools and stepladders to illustrate the world whose outlines Sue had drawn.

"This is India," she would say and, with a piece of

charcoal, blacken its long frontier. "Put in a temple." Then she would explain temples and sketch one for them to copy. "All this is Africa," she said. "Draw some lions and giraffes. Like this." The sisters earmarked France with Eiffel Towers, Ireland with shamrocks, Switzerland with edelweiss.

"Here is Mexico," Sue declared at last, weeks after the map had been started. "Where is Amapolas?" and the Gómez sisters chose a spot halfway down that was clear of the mountains already shaded in by Sue. This location and the space around it they quickly filled with all that was familiar, pigs, a rooster, a bicycle, a bus, an ear of corn, a sugar skull. Before long, these pictures overflowed into Texas on the north and Guatemala on the south.

When Padre Miguel had called on Sue in June, he examined the map, asked for a pencil, and, in the middle of the blank boot of Italy, drew in the dome, facade, and courtyard of Saint Peter's. He put down his pencil, picked it up again, and added on the right the Pope's balcony and His Holiness upon it. Then, with a wave, he walked past France, Spain, Portugal, the Atlantic Ocean, and out the door.

AT TEN O'CLOCK that Friday evening, while the town of Amapolas slept (with the exception of Blas Arriaga, still hungry and haranguing in the square), Sue left her house with the door unlocked and stood in the lane outside her wall. The air, cool and clear, carried no hint of rain. She noticed that Herr Otto's house, directly opposite her own, was full of light. Through one of its *sala* windows, Sue saw the musician and his sister at the piano.

Madame Anna had arrived six months ago and, without wasting a moment, torn her brother's solitude to shreds. At that time he began to be seen in public, at the post office, and at the widow Avila's store, and even in the church one day, advising Padre Miguel about the rehabilitation of the organ.

Madame Anna was an actual widow, as Ursula Bowles had been, separated from her husband by death, rather than, as in the cases of Sue Ames and Frances Bowles, by pain and rage. She came to Mexico from Brussels and changed for dinner every night, into chiffon and pearls and French-heeled slippers. The details of her past, like Herr Otto's, remained undisclosed, but the people of Amapolas were aware of a seventy-year-old radiance that lit up all the places where she went. Accompanied by her brother, she sang arias in his *sala* and, occasionally, the music of Bach and Handel in the church.

On this August night, Sue observed her through the open window beside her brother's long black piano and listened to her sing, while he played, a vaguely familiar folksong in one of the vaguely familiar languages they both spoke.

Sue walked on, cheered by the unexplained presence of

Madame Anna here on the hill at Amapolas, by her light step, her light laugh, and her light coloratura voice.

Continuing past Fran Bowles's silent, unlit house, Sue arrived soon after at Ursula's familiar gate, against which Lázaro Serrano now sat, wrapped in his frayed *sarape*, his lined face and stained teeth obscured both by the night and the wide brim of his hat.

Sue approached him, guided by the red ember of his cigarette, identifiable by its fumes as a Delicado.

"*Buenas noches*," they both said, and Sue asked, "Are you well?"

Lázaro, ignoring rheumatism, a chronic cough, and old tuberculosis scars, said, "Of course," and, as if she might have aged and sickened since they last met five days ago, inquired, "And you?"

In return, Sue said, "The same," though, in the erratic light of his lantern, each thought the other appeared less robust than when last seen.

"You will be at the inauguration of the *kiosco* in the plaza on Sunday," she remarked, and he nodded.

"Until dark," he said, and looked across the mesa at the night-shrouded province under his protection. "After that I must be here at my post, preventing crimes against these fourteen houses."

"Has there been a crime?"

Lázaro shook his head. "But one must always be prepared," he said. "Especially in the case of the property of the rich." He surveyed the houses he must guard, a number of which were unoccupied. "Ground squirrels, field mice, and a skunk have been known to enter." He gazed again over the flat expanse that was the Lomas de Amapolas. Sue, also, surveyed as much as she could see of the mesa.

"This is a beautiful place to live," she remarked to Lázaro, who disregarded the comment, made as it was by a woman who was also a foreigner.

Behind them, as they stood together under a quarter moon, the house of the widow Bowles stood locked, shuttered, and untenanted, on the edge of the bluff. For, in the end, the widow's estate had remained uncomplicated by an elusive heir. Six weeks after her own death, it was discovered that her school friend Clara Daggett had died in her sleep a few months earlier. So the house and its bright, fragrant garden had reverted to Fran Bowles, who in due course sold it to Don Enrique Ortiz de León. Don Enrique let it be known that he had plans to resell it, but, so far, it still stood empty.

Lázaro and his blanket and chipped mug occupied the kitchen of Ursula's house, where he slept on the floor in front of the stove from dawn until noon. Then he awoke, drank his bitter coffee, and ate a sweet roll delivered warm from the baker by his grandson, Julián. Lázaro was seventy-five, Julián not more than seven.

"I saw Julián this morning," Sue told the watchman now. "He was pulling a small dog in a box on wheels through the plaza."

"I should have killed that dog with the rest of the litter." Lázaro dropped the stub of his cigarette to the ground and stepped on it. "Its mother, intended by God to feed her young, is dead. Now Julián gives this animal milk from his own cup and rice from his plate."

Sue had recently sketched an impression of Julián and his dog and propped it against the wall above her desk. This meant that each time she crossed the room the eyes of the fragile-boned child and his frail creature followed her passage. The animal, almost too young to stand, occupied a wooden crate not much larger than a cigar box. To this carrier four wheels and a length of rope had been attached. Sue understood that someone had helped Julián build this cart. Not his father, who was in jail for attacking a relative, nor his mother, who had become pregnant again while still nursing the last of her five children, nor his brothers, who were all under six.

"Until Sunday, then," Sue reminded Lázaro, and turned back in the direction of her house.

Arriving at the wall that enclosed Frances Bowles's trees and hardy plants, Sue gave way to impatience. It is wrong of Fran to be absent now, with workmen to be directed and decisions to be made. It is her mother who will be honored on Sunday, not mine.

A letter from her own mother had arrived yesterday. It began, "Darling," and Sue knew this was how her mother actually felt. Loving, uncritical, and unaware as a child, her longing was to arrange or rearrange circumstances, so that Sue would be as happy as she believed she herself had been at thirty-three. She and Sue's father, existing in the comfortable climate of lifelong acceptance, could scarcely recognize the absence of it among others.

"Darling, how is your painting?" Sue's mother would ask. "We ran into Tim the other day—still unmarried." Or, "Tim came home for a weekend with his family. He is becoming quite famous with his climbing." Yesterday's message was, "Your father and I are coming to Mexico again in a few months. Can you meet us in Guadalajara? Or shall we come to you and see your house at last?" Then, further on, "I have heard that Tim will return from Argentina (Mount Aconcagua) by way of Mexico (volcanoes). Have you had another showing? Sold more pictures?"

Once inside her house, Sue found the only four letters from Tim she had saved during her six-year residence in Mexico and, together with her mother's latest communication, deposited them on the kitchen table. After that, she left the house as she always did, regardless of the hour, at the end of the day. She admitted to herself that this habit had become a ritual, as though repose depended on it, and she could not sleep without feeling a current of night air on her face, smelling the earth and the green of her garden,

The
Bandstand
in the
Square
....

207

acknowledging, without seeing them, the lake and the village below.

HOURS LATER, SUE lay awake, tormented by a sense of dereliction. She associated this with the problems of the bandstand in the square. What if Fran Bowles failed to appear at all, either to supervise the final construction or, simply, to celebrate her mother by her presence?

Oh, Fran, she silently rebuked her friend. Must you upset everything because of another man? Especially this one. And Sue remembered the archaeologist Fran had brought to the wedding of Altagracia Gómez and Bud Loomis. A rusty, dusty man, as Sue recalled, with a lined face and a wrinkled raincoat. A man older than Fran and older, too, than the three former objects of her passion, her two divorced husbands and Paco Alvarado. Fran sees in this man something besides excavations and shards, Sue realized.

She lay straight and still beneath her sheet, allowing her mind to wander at large among the places she had lived in and the people she had known. She reexamined dresses she had worn, teachers' comments on her work, a white rat she once owned. She thought of men she had met, those on mountaintops, in graveyards, or alphabetically arranged on the pages of school yearbooks.

At this point, Sue rose from bed, lit a lamp, and, consulting the letters on the kitchen table, began to mark the summits of the mountains Tim had climbed. One by one, and quite accurately, she entered the Eiger in Switzerland, Mont Blanc in France, Mount Kilimanjaro in Africa, Mount Karakoram in Nepal, and Fujiyama in Japan. Then, in case he had actually come to Latin America and begun in Argentina, she drew Mount Aconcagua. Beside each of the peaks, she printed an approximate date and painted a crimson pennant.

By now it was three o'clock Saturday morning. Once more in bed and still awake, she realized that in five hours she must be dressed, alert, and authoritative in the square.

AT EIGHT O'CLOCK Sue entered the plaza. Here the mason and his son sat silent at one end of a bench and the painter at the other, as if, though all three were born in this town, they had never met. When Sue's car appeared, they rose and started toward her, certain that in her North American way, by means of argument or money, she had obtained sections of stone and cans of paint in quantities sufficient for the completion of this job and probably two more like it.

Sue regarded the bandstand, a miniature copy of a grander version she had seen sometime, somewhere, perhaps in Lisbon or Versailles.

"Where is the foreman?" she asked the three men, and

one after another they said, "His godfather is sick in Rancho Verde," and, "Not expected to live," and, "As godson, he must take charge." In this way Sue learned that she must count on herself to supervise the completion of the *kiosco*.

She addressed the mason's son, a seventeen-year-old with the adobe of the jail still under his fingernails. "Please find Patricio Gómez and bring him here," and five minutes later her gardener was at her side, presenting a solution.

"When I go to La Luz in your car to make arrangements with a mariachi band, I will drive a short distance out of my way to the stoneworks, to see if the missing section of the balustrade is there, waiting only to be delivered. After that, I will engage the musicians for four o'clock tomorrow and on the way back pick up three cans of black paint."

He is remarkable, Sue realized, as Patricio proceeded to dismiss the three workmen, telling them to eat at noon and be back here ready to work at one. Long ago, she had perceived Patricio to be an instinctive leader. Was it because of his place as eldest son in the Gómez family? Or was it the result of experience he had gained while resolving the perplexities of the three North American women who, in one way or another, fell under his supervision?

Returned to her house on the hill, with Patricio already traveling south, Sue took coffee, an orange, and a roll to the edge of her terrace, stretched out in a long chair, and closed her eyes. A mild warmth enveloped her from a sun still low in the east, a bird she failed to identify released a few measures of song over her head, and some animal, a lizard or a field mouse, crept behind her. The satisfying smells of mint and chives rose from the pots at her side. She had started to peel her orange when sounds erupted from the front of the house. There was an angry knock on her door, followed at once by others. She ignored them all. Then came the heavy tread of boots, first on the garden path, then closer, on the bricks of the terrace where she sat. Still holding the orange, her eyes still shut, she listened as a visitor reached her side. She heard a voice.

"Where in hell have you been?" Then Bud Loomis, standing between her and the sun so that his shadow fell across her, went on, "I can't meet the damn tax deadline," and now Sue, opening her eyes, saw something new in his. Defeat. Unconditional defeat of the sort that has to be made public.

She said, "Sit down," and brought him coffee.

"Maybe if we could have sold those last six lots," he said. "Maybe if the bank had given me another loan," and Sue watched him turn to stare at the ring of hills and the inactive volcano on the horizon.

"I've lost the whole goddamn place," Bud said, "every damn thing we built from scratch. Jesus," and he went on staring in the direction of the hills.

At this, Sue, as though witness to a revelation, experienced a pang. Is it possible, she asked herself, that this man, coarse-grained, acquisitive, amoral, ugly, feels as I do about these ten Mexican acres and the Mexican landscape around them? She searched his face for confirmation and found none.

Without looking at her, Bud spoke again. "Do you want to buy me out?" he said, and finally faced her.

Sue stared into his baffled eyes. She saw him thinking, Why me? Why the hell me?

"I don't have the capital," she said. "And I'm not good at business." And now the reality of her situation as co-developer of the property Bud knew as Poppy Heights struck her, sharp as a blow, and left her confounded. Unable to take her eyes from Bud's enraged profile, she began to miss him in advance. Foreseeing the consequences of his withdrawal, Sue sank, unresisting, into the quicksand of anxiety. This was simply too much, on top of everything else. On top of the water shortage and the disease that was killing the children. On top of the unfinished bandstand and Fran Bowles's irresponsible absence, her own nagging concern about the disposition of the widow Bowles's ashes, and all the rest. What do I mean by that? Sue asked herself. What is "all the rest"?

Now Bud was walking to the terrace wall. There followed a pause.

"I guess I'll have to go to Don Enrique," Bud said. "I've got to have that dough in thirty days."

He left and Sue peeled her orange. She ate her hard roll.

The
Bandstand
in the
Square

....

213

PATRICIO GÓMEZ RETURNED to Sue's house at one o'clock. He said, "Bad news."

"What is it?" she asked, and, as though it might alter his message, reminded him that the three workmen were waiting in the square.

"The missing stone piece is nowhere to be found," Patricio said. "The *maestro* will have a duplicate ready in three weeks." Seeing her face, he added, "I have the paint, however. The mason and his son can help the painter and, together, the three can finish that work this afternoon." Aware that she was still not satisfied, he reassured her. "Meanwhile I will close the aperture with woven rope."

"Thank you," Sue said, and asked about the musicians.

"There you have my good news." Now Patricio exposed his white teeth in a smile, and, for an instant, Sue imagined she heard him hum a tune.

"Señora," he said. "For this occasion I have engaged the best mariachi group in La Luz. The best musicians with the best voices and the best instruments. All ten of them," and he was pleased to perceive that the young señora, who smiled less and less these days, now, for the time being, appeared happy.

She said, "At least we have them. Now I will go to the plaza for an hour or two to supervise the painting," and, because Saturday was the day of the outdoor fruit market, went into the kitchen to find her basket. Patricio, following her, immediately noticed the recent additions to the map.

He said, "What is all this?" and pointed to the mountain summits decorated with flags.

"Various mountains." Sue was already at the door.

"Why have you marked these peaks?"

"Because I know someone who has climbed them."

Patricio was impressed. He shook his head, first in disbelief, then in admiration, and walked the length of the map again. Finally he returned to stand before Mexico, crowded with drawings between its two seas and two frontiers. Patricio examined this map and, with some difficulty, located the central mountain range, partially obscured by the children's representations of snakes and birds.

"There is no flag on Popocatépetl. Here." He placed his finger on the spot.

"The person who climbed the others has not yet tried Mount Popo," Sue said. Then, without a pause, "We have no time for this. Three workmen are waiting in the square."

SUE, SPENDING AN hour or two on a bench in front of the bandstand, saw all at once details of Sunday's celebration as if it were in progress now, a day ahead of time. Without difficulty she was able to see everyone she knew, dancing. Moving in and out of view, glided Don Enrique and his Leni, the doctor and his fiancée, who was a nurse in La Luz, Bud Loomis, in close step with Altagracia. Now Herr Otto circled into sight with his sister, who was dressed in dove-gray silk, as if for a gavotte. Fran Bowles, miraculously returned in time, was wheeling slowly in the arms of her archaeologist.

Who am I to dance with? Sue asked herself in a reversion to adolescent panic, and, for a few seconds, as she sat alone on a concrete bench that advertised Dos Equis beer in the plaza of Amapolas, remembered dancing school.

Seized by dread, she might as well have been sitting on one of Miss Parson's stiff-backed rented chairs as here on this hard slab in Mexico, nodding to passersby. At Miss Parson's, an unknown twelve-year-old boy, forcibly propelled in her direction, stopped in front of her and uttered the words, "May I have this dance?" They had danced, the afternoon had eventually ended, and Sue never saw this particular savior again.

Interrupting this recollection, a young man eating purple ice from a stick joined her on the bench. It was Blas Arriaga, the hunger striker. Blas said the flavor was grape and very good. If she wished a *paleta*, he would call the vendor, who was wheeling his refrigerated container down the street.

Sue shook her head. "Did your strike have good results?"

she asked Blas, and he said that yes, the newspaper in La Luz had included a picture of him on the second page of its second section.

"And not only that, señora," he went on. "There is talk of an investigation into the entire water situation in this town. A commission has already been appointed."

"Good," Sue said, and watched while Blas licked his stick clean and tossed it onto the path.

"Until tomorrow afternoon, then," she said, and rose to thank the painters.

"Surely, the *kiosco* will be dry by morning," she remarked, as if it were an established fact.

"You may tie up your vines after the first hour of sun," one of the painters told her, and the other two nodded.

In the space left by the missing section of stonework, Patricio's interwoven and knotted ropes formed the net he had promised to protect the unwary from a fall. Sue believed she had seen pictures of such nets used in lion and tiger traps.

She was about to enter her car when the watchman's grandson Julián, pulling the wheeled box with his month-old dog inside, stopped beside her.

"Your animal must enjoy these excursions," Sue said insincerely, and the boy, his hand placed firmly on the animal's head to prevent a leap for freedom, nodded.

Exactly how old is this child? Sue wondered, and she tried to guess his age by the size of his bare feet, flaked with drying mud.

With the door of her car half-open, her basket still empty on the seat, Sue followed the boy's short progress to the corner, where the ice cream vendor had stopped in the street to make change. Julián was pulling his homemade wagon in a wide circle around this obstacle when a motorcycle carrying the cobbler's twin teenage nephews careened around the corner, causing the child to jump aside in time to see his animal and its makeshift vehicle crushed.

Confusion ensued at the corner. The twins paused, observed what they had done, shook their heads, and, a little off balance, rode on. The *paleta* vendor hastily pushed his wheeled freezer onto the narrow sidewalk, followed by two women with children clinging to their skirts. A crowd of unlikely mourners surrounded the small corpse.

Out of this turmoil and into the middle of the street walked Julián, alone. Looking neither left nor right, he departed the scene without a sound or a backward glance or even a splinter of wood to remind him that he had owned this animal.

Sue, about to get into her car, saw an image of herself running after the child and loudly calling out, "Cry, can't you? Cry!"

ON THE MORNING of the dedication of the bandstand, Sue woke to voices, a man's and a woman's, on Fran's terrace, which stretched almost to her own. Laughter and the sound of coffee cups confused her, and for a moment she was back in Santa Prisca, on a balcony of the Hotel Miranda, listening to talk from the adjoining quarters. And today, five years later, in this different place, one of these voices was still Fran's. The other, deeper and less erratic than Paco's, must belong to Fran's latest friend, Carter Riley. They must have come back in the middle of the night, Sue realized, and she felt the weight of care slide smoothly from her. Perhaps, together, they can save this day, or part of it, at least.

An hour later, the three sat in the partial shade of Sue's olive tree and talked.

"We have problems," Sue said, and began to list them.

It was now, as she presented these dilemmas, that her respect for this man, Carter Riley, took root and began to grow. By the time the sun stood over them at noon, she had forgotten his reserve and his indifference to climates, clothes, and the relation between them. She was no longer bothered by his formerly annoying habit of pulling at one ear when he thought. Aware that he was an archaeologist, she had, until today, harbored a dislike of the earthy aura that she imagined clung to him.

This morning, prejudice vanished. Addressing the problems one by one, Carter Riley offered solutions to them all.

"The wild-animal net must be replaced," and he looked around him. "What about these?" and he pointed to three of Sue's heavy clay pots, planted last January, by lucky chance, with roses now in flower.

"The paint on the wrought iron will be dry," he pronounced. "Where are the vines you want planted?" and Sue explained they were barely surviving in a cluster of cans under an ash tree in the plaza.

"I'll plant them," Carter said. "I've got a shovel in the car."

He looked north, then east, to see Sue's view. "All of it, everything in sight, is pure Mexico," he said. "Have there been discoveries of Indian caves?" And then, before either of the women could answer, he asked out of context, "What about music?"

Sue, happy to report on a matter already settled, explained that a mariachi band of ten from a bar in La Luz had been engaged by Patricio Gómez and was expected to arrive at three o'clock, an hour before the interim mayor's opening speech.

"Where is the regular mayor?" Fran asked, and Sue described the accident on the front seat of the official's old Pontiac.

The three sat for a few minutes without speaking in the

*The
Bandstand
in the
Square*

....

219

green stillness of the flower beds. Then Sue, calling on her waning energy, turned to face Frances Bowles.

"There is something else," she said. "Your mother's ashes."

When Fran answered, her voice was full of relief. "It's been so much on my mind. But what can we do?" she asked Sue. "The whole town will be looking on."

They had forgotten Carter. He said, "What is it? Can I help?" and five minutes later the archaeologist had the facts. He knew that months earlier, in April, when Fran was in Chiapas or Yucatán, all three Gallegos brothers, the undertakers from La Luz, had visited the mesa at Amapolas and, failing to find the widow's daughter, had sought out Sue Ames.

They found her on her terrace, painting rows of corn, the slopes of an extinct volcano. The brothers, in their polished black shoes and their dark suits, which were warm for April, explained that they had tried to cooperate with the widow's daughter—had, in fact, waited four months for her to claim these remains—and now, under the laws of propriety, must deliver them for their ultimate disposal.

"She wants them scattered on a mountain in New Mexico," Sue told them, using the present tense. "Somewhere near her husband's."

Confronted in this way by North American barbarity, the brothers had nothing to say. Instead, they walked to the wall at the edge of the mesa and looked down on the cemetery.

"Here is a graveyard," one said.

"And consecrated," said another.

"I cannot take responsibility," Sue said, and she would have gone on, but Padre Miguel, stopping for an afternoon call and hearing voices, came around the corner of the house and joined the group.

As soon as he understood the problem, the priest announced that he would take charge of the matter, and he escorted the three undertakers in their black shoes and black suits to their dust-covered black car.

"We cannot wait indefinitely for the Señora Francisca," the parish priest told Sue, and, within a day or two, all that remained of Ursula Bowles, except for what people remembered of her, which was first history, later on imagination, was buried in the village *panteón*. Not actually within the Catholic confines of the cemetery but on its boundary, where only a surveyor with instruments could have said whether she was inside or out. The morning glories that sprang up in the graveyard after the first June rain had flourished, and Ursula's ashes rested under one of these shallow lakes of blue.

Now Carter, his eyes on the widow's grave, was making calculations. Finally he spoke. "Let me take care of

everything. After midnight tonight. No one will know."
He stared down at the site. "All those flowers," he said.

A FEW HOURS later, when Sue was about to
change from denim into white linen, Patricio Gómez
knocked on her door to say that the three o'clock bus had
arrived, bringing more people than usual to Amapolas.
Then he continued, as though on second thought, "The
ten musicians are not among them."

When Sue said nothing, Patricio examined her face and
realized that the words had yet to be invented that would
describe her disappointment. For a long moment neither
spoke.

At last Patricio said, "Consider this, señora. Musicians
are to be found everywhere in Mexico. They are polishing
their instruments and waiting for your call even here, in a
town like this, with inadequate streetlights and insufficient
drainage." And he went on to name a number of local
artists who played guitars and violins. Then, after a moment
of thought, he remarked, "I know one musician who is
actually in Amapolas at this time and free to play this
afternoon."

"Who?" Sue asked, and her *chargé d'affaires* said,
"Aparicio Fuentes."

She had no recollection of this man. "What is his instrument?" she asked, and Patricio said, "The trumpet. Aparicio's instrument is the trumpet."

At this, Sue admitted defeat. There was nothing more she could do.

Patricio was waiting at the door. Moving away, Sue called over her shoulder, "Please ask Aparicio to be at the bandstand at three-thirty."

Before leaving, Sue stood for a moment in the kitchen in front of the map of Mexico. She found it to be so penciled and inked and crayoned that the only space left was on the undecorated rim of Popocatépetl.

AS SOON AS Sue reached the plaza, her forebodings began to dissipate. More people than she had expected filled the benches or bought ice cream or Orange Crush from vendors. Padre Miguel sat by himself on a bench, tapping one foot to his own beat, as though he heard dance music in advance. But would there be dancing? So far, no musician had appeared. The nearby street corner, scene of yesterday's accident involving the boy Julián and his dog, had been invaded by two beggars from out of town.

Peace, like shade in an April drought, calmed Sue when she inspected the bandstand. The flowerpots transferred here by Carter Riley filled the empty space in the balustrade as if they were part of the original design. The bougainvilleas, stricken but still alive, had been untangled, planted, and tied to the freshly painted iron.

She looked about for Carter, to thank him, but here in front of her was Patricio, trailed by an exceedingly tall, exceedingly thin young man wearing sideburns and carrying a trumpet. Sue Ames extended her hand.

"This is the musician you have hired," Patricio told her, and pushed Aparicio Fuentes forward.

"Today's program is to inaugurate the bandstand and to honor the widow Bowles," she told him, and he replied, "At your orders."

"There must be an introduction to the speeches."

"*A sus órdenes*," said Aparicio.

"Followed by accompaniment while the guests visit and inspect the *kiosco*."

"*A sus órdenes*."

"After that, there may be dancing."

"Dancing," and the musician, without playing it, lifted the trumpet to his lips.

It was precisely at this moment that Sue Ames fell out of touch with reality. Logic and the lessons of experience collapsed at their foundations and were replaced by a past grown hazy and a present too insubstantial to examine. Fantasy hung about her and obscured her vision of the village square. She struggled to recover clear sight.

"What sort of music do you play?" she asked Aparicio,

who, as though he had joined her in dreaming, answered, "All."

At this particular time, with the ceremony in the plaza not yet under way, four vehicles approached Amapolas, one from each major compass point. From the east came the mule-drawn cart of a farmer who raised chickens and hoped to sell a few in the square. From the west, on a bus, came Padre Miguel's aunt, bringing him a two-layer box of molasses candy. Nearing the scene of festivities from the south was the Volkswagen of the mayor's brother-in-law, on his way to remove his sister, nieces, and nephews from gossip and scandal. The car that would arrive from the north was a Jeep driven by, as his tourist card attested, a North American male. Both car and driver appeared bruised. If the highway patrol had stopped this man to examine his permit, they would have discovered not only his name but his age, thirty-seven, and his marital status, divorced. If they had interrogated him, he might have asked them where he was. For this foreigner with a cut cheek had been given wrong directions twice within an hour. Like the mayor's brother-in-law, he should have come to Amapolas from the south.

It was almost six when he reached the arrow that pointed to the town. He wasted five minutes more on the mesa, knocking at doors that no one opened, ready with questions no one heard. He proceeded then down the hill to the

The
Bandstand
in the
Square
....
225

village plaza, drawn by the sound of a trumpet and some lights. When he saw the gathering of people, he parked his car at the curb.

Patricio Gómez, observing the festivities from the sidewalk, watched this car stop and moved to inspect it. Only then did he see the coils of a rope, a pick, and an ax in the rear and understand there would soon be a flag on Mount Popo. For that reason he walked around the vehicle and opened the door on the driver's side. For that reason he said, "She is dancing," and pointed. "Over there."

NOW, FOR MORE than an hour, the plaza had been washed in silver by music. The cobblestones, the housefronts, the trees, the people, and their animals shone with it. The sound Aparicio drew from his trumpet was as pure as air never breathed, as transparent as ice. It could fill the plaza with its volume or bind listeners with a thread finer than silk. And Aparicio had not lied when he said he played everything.

He knew all the music ever written, from the national anthem to opera arias. No request from the celebrants in the square was refused. He knew the compositions of Bizet, Sousa, and Josef Strauss. He knew the homesick songs of his native land, as well as those of love denied.

Sue's fears had proved groundless. She had moved about the floor with men she knew and didn't know for an hour.

She was being led in sweeping turns by Don Enrique Ortiz de León when a long-unheard voice, speaking from behind her, asked permission to cut in.

A NUMBER OF people looked for Sue after that and inquired of Patricio, "Where is the Señora Sue?"

"The mountain climber arrived," he told them. "First he invited her to dance. Then he offered to drive her home."

LONG BEFORE MIDNIGHT the lights were out in the plaza. Nevertheless, a radiance persisted there until dawn. As soon as the festivities were over, the mayor's wife and children emerged into the shimmering mist to flee Amapolas and hide somewhere else. Padre Miguel, affected by this mist, hesitated on the steps, then entered the church to pray, for throughout the evening of light and sound he had longed to dance.

Aparicio Fuentes had reached home by now and wrapped his instrument in a torn strip of red velvet. He slept as well as anyone else in Amapolas that night, after the inauguration by trumpet of the bandstand in the square.

As It
Happened

....

As it happened, all five houses of the foreigners on the mesa above Amapolas were abandoned before the next December 12th, which was Guadalupe Day. In that space of time and in good order, the strangers, one or two at a time, departed. First to leave, involuntarily, was Ursula Bowles, and last, by choice, Sue Ames.

It was in October, with the corn still green as summer in the fields, that Herr Otto von Schramm entrusted his Steinway concert grand piano for the second time to Pancho Moreno and his splintering truck and followed it by taxi to La Luz. As the cab pulled away, Herr Otto lowered his window to bow to Sue, who was standing outside her wall

228

to see him go. Madame Anna, from the seat beside him, leaned forward to wave a kid-gloved hand. At that moment the particular silence induced by the cessation of music spread east to west from one house to another on the hill.

One morning two weeks later, Bud Loomis loaded his pickup truck and transferred his desk and bed, his cooking pots and painted plates, along with his wife and son, to the location one hour beyond La Luz where he would become associated, for the second time, with property development.

It came about in the end that, of all the expatriates on the mesa at Amapolas, only Bud Loomis failed to separate himself from this part of Mexico in the middle of the country, these plains and rises and desert stretches that surrounded the city of La Luz. Long before he became a permanent resident of Mexico, Bud could often be found standing at some chosen spot, a reservoir, a grain silo, a trench between rows of corn, where he would say to anyone who listened, "This is my *tierra*," failing to roll the *r*'s.

Frances Bowles turned her back permanently on her house above the graveyard and the town early in December. This final departure followed a short absence that occurred during the month of November. On that occasion, Carter Riley went along.

He and Fran turned north at the paved highway and traveled for two days in the direction of New Mexico.

There they drove back and forth at the foot of the Sangre de Cristo Mountains, and early on their second morning, when Fran said, "Here," followed Ursula's instructions and consigned the contents of the copper box Carter had disinterred to a brisk canyon wind.

Not long after this, Fran, assisted by Carter Riley, labeled her desk and chairs, her typewriter and stove, her handwoven curtains and bedspreads, and watched them hauled away in midafternoon by Pancho Moreno and his truck. All of these things were directed to an address in San Cristóbal de las Casas in Chiapas, their chosen headquarters for jungle forays.

In her nearly empty house Fran offered Carter sandwiches. "Sit down for a few minutes," she insisted.

But the minutes stretched to an hour, and by the time sweaters, shoes, and a number of *rebozos* were in her suitcase, night had fallen. Fran was wrapping the portrait of a saint painted on tin, when a power failure occurred and the lights went off. They finished packing by the gleam of half a dozen candles, which Carter pinched out as they left.

Toward the end of the same December week, Sue Ames, traveling alone, left Amapolas in the same car she had arrived in six years before. Tim, her husband, former and to be, had preceded her in the direction of a cliff in Utah. Sue, driving over landscape too familiar to memorize, scarcely noticed the leafless trees and unseeded fields. Here and there the letters GDO appeared on *bodega* walls and silos. The president of Mexico, Gustavo Díaz Ordaz, had already served four years of his six-year term, and his initials had weathered. Two years from now, in 1970, they would be painted over to make room for the first letters of the next president's name. Letters I may never see, Sue told herself, with an almost unprecedented instinct for the future.

IT WAS DUSK when files of pilgrims first appeared, singing and carrying lanterns along the edges of the highway. When Sue chose December 12th to leave her house, she had forgotten it was Guadalupe Day. Now, with columns of weary faithful on each side, she stared into the vast obscurity, searching for the invisible chapel at whose invisible altar they would pray.

IN AMAPOLAS, THE townspeople watched the exodus of the householders without surprise. If they themselves had been forced to leave this place because of lack of food or money, they would have returned here as soon as matters improved. But in the case of the North Americans and two Europeans who came and went, there was no such simple reason for either their arrival or departure.

"My church never became central to their lives," Padre Miguel remarked. "They came rarely, and then only to listen to the organ or contemplate the colonial art."

"They are saddened by so much disease," the intern said. "They want to live where every house has a working toilet and garbage is collected and taken out of sight."

Don Enrique knew it was not these things that drew the strangers away from the hill. It was his opinion that, in coming here, they had moved too far from the dwellings and graves of their ancestors.

"One must not discard the legacy of one generation to the next," he would remark to his secretary, Leni, as he stood at his front door, one hand on worn stone, the other on ancient oak. "Their roots are shallow from frequent transplanting," he told her, and she would put his words down on the notepad she carried about with her. For Don Enrique was bringing his family history up to date by writing his autobiography. To effect the orderly completion of this project, he had installed Leni in the house that had belonged to Ursula Bowles. A number of evenings were devoted to this work. On these occasions, the author would escort his secretary to the gate, where they would exchange a few words with Lázaro, the watchman, now moved to cement-block quarters of his own just inside the *hacienda* wall.

"Until tomorrow, then," Don Enrique would call after her pleasant, undistinguished form as she picked her way home across an empty field. Then he would return, occasionally for the second time that evening, to the thin mattress of his great-grandmother's canopied four-poster bed.

One afternoon in November, when Tim Ames and Carter Riley were both in residence, Don Enrique delivered a lunch invitation to Sue, as well as one to Fran Bowles next door.

"Of course, the gentlemen are included," the heir to the *hacienda* told them.

The fact was that neither he nor anyone else in the village knew exactly how to classify the two men. Fran Bowles had made no effort to explain the frequent presence of the archaeologist. Sue, on the other hand, had tried to clarify her situation.

"The Señor Ames and I were married for five years, then divorced," she told Patricio. "That is why I came to Amapolas."

"In that case, which are you now? Married or divorced?"

"Both," Sue said.

Padre Miguel felt only relief that this union, which in God's eyes had never been dissolved, was still functioning as well as ever.

"Señora," he said. "Your marriage is an example of the joy and peace to be found by two mature people practiced in the art of communication."

Sue translated this remark to Tim, who was standing at

her side, and he bowed. Then, as if she had answered her husband's letters, she bowed, too.

On the occasion of Don Enrique's invitation, he handed each couple a page of instructions that included a rough map.

"Start early," he told them. "It is a two-hour drive from here to the *rancho*." Then he turned back from the door with further information. "We will eat in the field, *al fresco*."

On the appointed day, Carter offered the use of his van, and, with Fran Bowles beside him and Sue and Tim behind, drove up and down grades, around curves, and across flat stretches under a winter sun. The temperate morning light fell upon cattle grazing on stubble in pastures, goats knocking stones from hillsides, and burros roaming the paved roads, as well as on the peeling facades of farmhouses where birdcages hung on the front walls.

The North Americans soon noticed that every settlement, scattered, deprived, and undistinguished as it might be, was heralded by a road sign at its outskirts.

"How I love these names," Sue said, and recited a few. Corral de Piedras, El Caballo Muerto, Los Ricos, La Esperanza, La Malcontenta, turning them into English for the benefit of Tim Ames, who understood and spoke more Spanish than he permitted to be known.

Tim gazed now at his former wife. Ever since his arrival in Amapolas, he had watched this woman in wonder. Once or twice on his first night at her adobe house, he had almost asked her, "Have we met?" Was it merely her hair that was different, longer? Or was it her new habits, scrambling chiles into her eggs, for instance? Fascinated, he had looked at her drawings, which included several of him. Mesmerized, he examined the map on the kitchen wall. Now, in November, while Sue repeated names of hamlets, he studied her as if she were a history assignment.

At the end of two hours, as Don Enrique had predicted, the travelers arrived at the *rancho*. Its name was Los Bravos, according to the iron letters on the arch over its iron gates. To the right and left of this entrance, rolling into the distance, broad meadows extended as far as a hill, a stand of trees, and an arroyo. On these meadows, a number of black bulls peacefully grazed and wandered.

The luncheon guests stared. "A new project of Don Enrique's," Sue supposed, and Fran remarked that all these *hectáreas*, extending to the horizon, perhaps belonged to a de León or Ortiz cousin or in-law.

As it turned out later, they were both right. Don Enrique met them at the door of the pink fortress that stood at the end of the drive. "Almost three hundred years old," he told them, "and barely modified."

Now, from a smaller pink structure to the left, Bud Loomis, Altagracia Gómez, and their flawless child emerged to join the visitors, and, within half an hour, the entire matter of the bull ranch was made clear. Host and company sat in a courtyard shadowed by massive walls and drank local brandy while the sun hung at noon, as if waiting for news before moving ahead with the day.

"The husband of a cousin," Don Enrique began, "on my father's side . . . ," and went on to narrate at some length details of the Ortiz connection. "In any case," he said, at last, "this negotiation is a simple matter of trade between relatives. I have exchanged some of the property on the hill at Amapolas for a share of this endeavor, the breeding and raising of fighting bulls." With this, he lifted a hand, as if to prevent his audience from interrupting. "There is more," he said. "I will make a second investment here," and he raised an arm to encompass the structure looming behind him. "In this house," he said, "and in villas yet to be built, I intend to take paying guests." At this point he made a final announcement. "I have asked Señor Loomis to take charge of the construction of these guest quarters."

Silence fell again and continued until Sue raised her glass and said, "To Bud."

Within an hour, lunch was served at a table set on a cropped field behind the house. It was not quite three, but, by that time, the day had already begun to decline.

"How quickly the daylight shortens at November's end," Don Enrique said, and asked Altagracia to find shawls for the North American women's shoulders.

Chicken *mole*, bread, cheese, fruit, and wine were

brought and a number of toasts proposed and drunk. During the meal, a barnyard rooster pecked at crumbs between the guests' feet, emerging from time to time to strut and crow in full view of all those present. Near the end of the meal, one of the ranch dogs chased a ground squirrel under the table, almost upsetting it, causing a wineglass to fall.

"What in hell—?" Bud began, but the lunch guests were pushing back their chairs. By four, the shadow of the impregnable structure behind the picnickers had reached one end of the table and begun to creep across its length.

Now Sue rose to make her second toast of the day. "I propose a salute to Mexico," she said, as if a military unit had appeared to raise the national flag on a staff suddenly installed in front of the picnic party. At these words, all stood with lifted glasses and drank to the land they had either inherited for life or borrowed temporarily. Sue, with her glass still raised, stood silent for a drawn-out moment, as if she had prepared a speech and it had left her mind. Then, with the others, she turned away.

All that remained then was to inspect the animals that comprised the bone, sinew, and profits of Rancho Los Bravos.

The entire party set off across a field to stand at the heavy barrier that confined the bulls to their broad pastures. The quiet creatures, huge of shoulder, heavy of head, and slow to focus, ignored the visitors. But at the corral occupied by yearlings, things were different. The animals left off butting each other to approach the rail, where they remained, apparently in contemplation. Sue watched Bud, holding his son at shoulder height, face one of these young bulls across the barricade. The animal stared unblinking, in what might have been a challenge, into the pair of light blue eyes and the two enormous dark ones that stared back at him. Who is the enemy here? asked all these eyes.

"Now you will come to visit me in two places," Don Enrique said while farewells were being spoken.

But, as it happened, none of these four North Americans, after their departure a week or two later, ever returned to this part of Mexico again.

Frances Bowles, content with Carter Riley, followed him without hesitation from continent to continent, living at excavation sites where rain never came and at others where it never stopped.

Sue Ames, as far as anyone could see, adapted herself easily to change, painting what she chose, usually in places of much natural splendor, in the company of the reckless man she had left once and married twice.

OF THE FOREIGNERS who had lived on the mesa, only Sue, clinging to her five rooms, her olive trees, and her clumps of iris, refused to sell her house. Shaking her head, she listened to Don Enrique's proposition to knock down walls, combine her garden with Fran's, and link the two houses, which then could be occupied, all at once, by several generations of a family.

"Oh, no," she said. "I couldn't possibly sell it." And, years later, on those occasions when she was interviewed after a showing of her work and asked where she lived, she always answered, "I divide my time between Mexico and here," with a nod to wherever here at that moment happened to be.

Instead of renting to a stranger, she installed Patricio as caretaker of her house. At first he slept in the small bedroom off the kitchen. Then, in the course of time, he married and had children.

"Use whichever of the rooms you want," Sue wrote. "When I come, I will let you know in advance so that you and your family can move to the village, nearer your friends and the school." At the end of these letters, in which she included her latest address, she often added, "Send me news of Amapolas. I like to hear."

Then Patricio would send the news.

"*Estimada Señora,*" he would begin, and go on to tell her about the weather. "This has been the coldest winter in recent history. Two calves froze and children under five could walk on ice at the edge of the lake."

Or about public works. "The state authorities have hired ten men of the town to install a drainage system. Accordingly, trenches have been dug on almost every street of Amapolas and lengths of pipe laid ready beside them. But the officials failed to notify the townspeople that the connection to each house is the financial responsibility of the owner. So far, only six houses have been connected and the rest of the pipe is lying next to the ditches, which are now full of leaves and rubbish."

In another letter he announced, "There will soon be a new cemetery on the other side of the village. The old one is full."

Once he wrote about the view. "Señora, what is to be seen from the edge of your garden has changed. Now there is a limestone quarry at the foot of the hills to the north, and a road has been cut through the cornfields to accommodate the trucks. So now there is activity where before there was none."

Occasionally he reported on her garden. "*Estimada Señora*, this year's drought was more severe than usual and the first rose you planted here, the one that pleased you most, has died. The fruit trees, on the contrary, are producing plums, apricots, and especially figs in greater abundance than ever before." Then Patricio would go on, "But why tell you all these things? You have been absent so long you must have forgotten the place by now."

When this happened, Sue longed to summon him through space to stand before her.

You are wrong, Patricio, she wanted to say. She wanted to explain what she remembered. Listen, she imagined telling him. I can see everything as clearly now as I did then.

Perhaps more clearly. The children sliding on the ice, the first grave to be dug in the new graveyard, the unburied pipes, the trucks invading the fields—I see it all. And what is more, I hear the new church bell, the loudspeaker recently installed in the square, and the shot that killed the burro with the broken leg. I hear it all.

In the case of my garden, which I still know by touch, I celebrate the figs and mourn the Guadalupe rose. I hold the fruit and flower in my hand.

Consider that, Patricio. Consider that.

Books in the
Harvest American Writing Series

ARABIAN JAZZ
Diana Abu-Jaber

BABY OF THE FAMILY
Tina McElroy Ansa

CONSIDER THIS, SEÑORA
Harriet Doerr

THE CHOIRING OF THE TREES
Donald Harington

EKATERINA
Donald Harington

LET THE DEAD BURY THEIR DEAD
Randall Kenan

MESSENGER BIRD
Dan McCall

TALLER WOMEN: A CAUTIONARY TALE
Lawrence Naumoff

PATCHWORK
Karen Osborn

MARBLES
Oxford Stroud

BLUE GLASS
Sandra Tyler